'Are you going to tell Alex the truth?'

'No! *Never*.' Venetia said it so fiercely that Ginny stared at her, her lips parted in surprise.

'You have got it badly.'

'Yes, I suppose I have.' Venetia gazed down at her hands for a long moment before looking at Ginny with wide, vulnerable eyes. 'I've never felt this way about a man before.'

They stared at each other, realising that in this, as in so many things, they felt the same way.

'So it looks like stalemate,' Ginny said.

'Yes, I suppose it does,' Venetia agreed reluctantly.

TWIN
TORMENT

BY

SALLY WENTWORTH

MILLS & BOON LIMITED
ETON HOUSE   18-24 PARADISE ROAD
RICHMOND   SURREY   TW9 1SR

*First published in Great Britain 1991
by Mills & Boon Limited*

© Sally Wentworth 1991

*Australian copyright 1991
Philippine copyright 1991
This edition 1991*

ISBN 0 263 77259 4

*Set in Times Roman 10½ on 12 pt.
01-9110-52731 C*

Made and printed in Great Britain

CHAPTER ONE

IT FELT strange to be travelling alone. As Ginny pushed the luggage-trolley towards the checking-in desk at Heathrow Airport she tried to recall if she had ever made a journey without Venetia before. There had been odd day trips of course, with various friends and boyfriends, but nothing that you could call a real journey. But now here she was, flying off to Paris on a modelling assignment and feeling as if she'd forgotten something all the time.

There was already quite a long queue for the economy-class seats, but Ginny's agency had fixed a club-class seat and there were only a couple of people in front of her. When her turn came she went to heave the cases on to the weighing shelf, but a voice said, 'Let me,' and a man behind her moved forward to lift them on for her. She flashed him a grateful smile but had to immediately turn away to hand over her ticket.

'Smoking or non-smoking?' the girl in the blue British Airways uniform asked her.

'Non-smoking, please.'

The girl dealt with the ticket and handed it back with the boarding card. 'You'll be in seat eleven. Enjoy your flight.'

'Thank you.' Ginny put the things away and swung her bag on her shoulder, gave a brief nod to the man in the queue and then walked through to the less crowded departure lounge. Several people glanced at her as she went by, noticing her height first, and then the natural grace that came from her years of training, first as a dancer and then as a model. Today her slim, almost boyish figure was hidden beneath a long, loose-fitting woollen coat and she was wearing a wide-brimmed felt hat over rich brown hair that fell long and straight halfway down her back. An amused smile quirked her mouth when she saw the glances; if Venetia had been with her the people wouldn't have just glanced, they would have stopped and stared.

The smoothness of the check-in had given her plenty of time, so Ginny went into the duty free shop and amused herself by trying the various perfumes on her wrists before settling for two bottles of Obsession by Calvin Klein, one for herself and one for Venetia. It didn't even occur to her to get different perfumes; they always wore the same. Next she went to the bookshop and bought one of the glossy monthly fashion magazines, then found a seat and settled down to read it while she waited for the flight to be called.

The magazine held her attention for ten minutes or so, but then Ginny grew restless; it felt strange having no one at her side to talk to, no one to discuss the clothes pictured in the magazine with or to criticise or admire the models. She was excited and a little nervous, too, to be going on an assignment alone. It had never happened to either of them before. Closing the magazine, Ginny looked round the huge room and thought she recognised the man who had been behind her in the queue sitting a few rows away but facing her. He had a documents case open on the low table in front of him and was going through some papers, a slight frown of concentration between his eyes. A high-flying businessman who thought his time so precious that he couldn't relax for even a minute, Ginny decided sardonically, with all the wealth of experience of her twenty-one years.

He was good-looking, though, with thick dark hair and lean features. And only about thirty, she guessed. She studied him covertly for a few moments, noting the good cut of his suit and his long-fingered hands. They had a thing about hands, she and Venetia, believing that you could tell a lot about a person's character from their shape if it was a man, and from the nails if it was a woman. The man glanced up, as if aware that someone was watching him, and Ginny nonchalantly opened her magazine again without meeting his eyes, not wanting to give him the satisfaction of knowing she'd been looking at him.

The Paris flight was called shortly afterwards and the stewardess showed the club passengers to their seats.

'Shall I take your hat and coat?' the stewardess offered, and Ginny passed them over. She enjoyed the individual attention and was grateful for the extra legroom, but had mixed feelings when the man in the queue was shown to the seat next to hers.

'Hello again,' he said pleasantly.

Ginny nodded coolly and did up her safety strap. She supposed she ought to have guessed that he would be put next to her when he had been the next in line. Well, it was only a short flight, she thought philosophically; she could put up with his company for an hour so long as he didn't make a pass or bore her to death about his job for the whole journey. The plane taxied to the runway and the engines began to rev for that impossible dash into the sky. It occurred to Ginny that she had never flown alone before either and her hands tightened on the arm-rests.

'Excuse me.'

She turned reluctantly to look at the man in the next seat.

'I'm sorry to bother you,' he said apologetically, 'but the thing is, I'm scared to death of flying. Would you mind very much if I held your hand?'

'What?' She gave him an astonished glance, looking for mockery in his face, but just then the plane began to tear down the runway and she grabbed his hand. 'Yes, of course. Hold on as tight as you like.'

He must have been scared because he held on to her hand until they were well up into the sky and were flying straight and level.

'You should be OK now,' Ginny pointed out when he still didn't let go.

'Mm? Of course. Thanks. I hope I haven't done you a permanent injury?' he remarked, turning her hand over to look at it.

Ginny noticed nail marks on the back of his and thought it was probably the other way round. 'I'll live.' She firmly removed her hand from his grasp and noticed a glint of amusement in the man's eyes, cool grey eyes with a hint of steel in their depths. 'Are you sure you're afraid of flying?' she asked suspiciously.

'Petrified,' he assured her, but he didn't look it.

Ginny gave a reluctant smile but turned to answer the stewardess who was asking her what she would like to drink. After they'd been served, both with gins and tonics, the man again turned to her. 'I bet you're going to Paris on business.'

'I could be going on holiday.'

He shook his head. 'No, if you were going on holiday you wouldn't be going alone; no one goes to Paris on holiday alone. Imagine walking through the *bois* or along by the Seine by yourself; nothing could be more melancholy.'

'I might want to be melancholy,' Ginny pointed out, a flicker of interest in her long-lashed hazel eyes.

Her neighbour grinned, an attractive grin that made his eyes crinkle. 'You're too young and too old to be melancholy.'

'How can I possibly be both?' she demanded, her eyebrows lifting.

'Adolescent youth and old age are the times to be melancholy; in between you just experience the good times and bad times of life.'

'You're quite a philosopher,' she remarked on a mocking note.

'You sound as if you don't approve. But then, most women don't like to be analysed.'

It was a provocative statement and there was a hint of challenge in his voice and in the slight raising of his left eyebrow. Ginny considered whether to take it up. He obviously expected her to. Perhaps it was his regular line, pushing the girl into getting into a debate with him so that he could get to know her. And to judge the level of her intelligence, of course. Was he the type who preferred brainy women, or dumb blondes? Ginny wondered. Her eyes went over him again and she caught the scent of his clean, fresh aftershave. Making a sudden decision, she accepted his challenge—but not quite in the way he obviously expected. 'And do men like to be analysed?' she returned. And, before he could answer, 'But of course they must; after all, men like nothing better than to talk about themselves, don't they?'

His grin widened and an arrested look came into his eyes. 'A fellow philosopher, no less.'

Ginny recognised that look; it was one she had seen in the eyes of men before and usually meant that they were attracted and would make a pass. But this man surprised her by leaning back in his seat and saying, 'And was I right—are you going to Paris on business?'

She nodded. 'Yes. And you are, of course.'

'On the principle that I'm travelling alone, too,' he said with a wry smile. 'You're half right. I am on a business trip, but not in Paris. I'm taking a connecting flight to Stockholm.'

'And do people go there alone for holidays?' Ginny asked mischievously.

He laughed. 'Not if they can possibly avoid it, especially in winter. It's much too cold.'

The stewardess came round again, offering them a meal that was halfway between breakfast and lunch. Her companion accepted his but Ginny counted up the calories in the fresh croissant and the omelette and fried potatoes and decided to settle for just coffee.

'Did you eat at home?' he asked her.

She shook her head. 'I'm being taken out to dinner when I get to Paris.'

Her neighbour's eyes ran over her slim figure in the modish dark green toreador-style trousers and jacket; the best outfit she and Venetia possessed. 'Are you in the fashion business?' he hazarded.

'I suppose you could say that. I'm a model—or at least I'm hoping to be one.'

His eyes widened with interest as she'd known they would. 'Are you going to do an audition or something? Do models have to do auditions?'

'Sometimes, if it's for clothes. But usually they're chosen from their photographs. Actually I was lucky to get this job,' Ginny confided. 'The crew was already over in Paris for a shoot when one of the models developed appendicitis and had to come home, so they needed a replacement with the same measurements and colouring quickly.'

'And you were chosen.'

'Well, it was a choice between me and one other girl.'

'But they picked you.'

Ginny gave a ghost of a smile and shook her head. 'No, we tossed for it.' It was the way she and Venetia had always settled the matter when a choice had to be made between them. Their father had started it when they were little girls and they had kept it up because it was the fairest way, although people had got so used to thinking of them as a pair that they seldom had to resort to it now except for chance things like this.

'You're very modest,' her companion remarked. He finished his meal and pushed the plate aside.

'You sound as if you didn't expect me to be.'

There was a challenge in Ginny's voice now and he laughed, recognising it. 'You're a refreshing change.'

It wasn't quite the compliment Ginny was used to but she found that she liked it. And she wasn't vain about her looks; how could she be when her exact double was always before her eyes? 'You must know some very conceited women, then.'

'Perhaps.' The lazy smile in his grey eyes gave nothing away.

Ginny found herself beginning to be intrigued by him and glanced at his left hand to see if he wore a wedding-ring, but the long fingers were bare. Looking up, she found him watching her and she flushed a little, realising from the amusement in his eyes that he knew why she'd looked. 'You said you were going to Stockholm on business,' she said hastily, hoping to distract him.

'That's right. I'm attending a conference there.'

'Really? On what subject?'

He gave her a brief look. 'Lasers. I'm a physicist.'

Ginny gulped; she hadn't the faintest idea what a physicist did. 'How interesting,' she murmured, and did a swift retake on her ideas about him. So he was a scientist and not a businessman. Somehow she liked that better. She had met many businessmen and didn't have any great opinion of them but she didn't know any scientists. 'Tell me about it,' she invited, with real curiosity in her tone.

'Well, it's an international symposium to discuss the application of laser materials in industry.'

'And you're going to take part in the discussion?'

'I'm going to read a paper, yes.'

Ginny looked at him for a long moment and then sighed. 'Just what is a physicist?' She stumbled over the word. 'Whoops. It's difficult even to say.'

He gave a crack of laughter that made other passengers turn to look at him. 'Another refreshing change; most people pretend they know all about the subject—and then go and look the word up in the dictionary, which doesn't help them at all.'

'So you tell me.' Ginny leaned nearer to him, her clear hazel eyes on his face.

He paused a moment, his eyes meeting hers, then said, 'Basically a physicist studies the properties of matter and energy: things like heat, light, sound, and electricity. Then there's also astrophysics, which deals with high-energy cosmic rays, for instance, and nuclear or atomic physics.'

Ginny sat up straight, her eyes widening. 'You don't make bombs, do you?'

His lips twitched at her reaction. 'No, my work is far more prosaic; I'm a lecturer in the physics department at a university. Going to one of these conferences is a perk that goes with the job.'

'More coffee, madam? Sir?' The stewardess came round again and they both had their cups refilled.

Ginny sat back in her seat, nursing her cup. She glanced out of the window. There was nothing to see but cloud, but it made her say, 'Do you go to a lot of these conferences, then?'

'Quite a few.'

'I suppose they have them all over the world; you must get to see some interesting places.'

'Yes, I've been quite lucky. They're often held in America or even Australia.'

Amusement shone in Ginny's eyes and she wrinkled her nose at him. 'And you so afraid of flying.'

He gave a delighted laugh. 'Well, I had to do *something* to break through that barrier of ice you'd put up.'

Ginny laughed too, her face lighting up, her eyes like sparkling jewels beneath her finely arched brows. Again an arrested look came into her companion's eyes, but it was even deeper this time. 'You haven't told me anything much about yourself,' he remarked. 'Do you live in London?'

'Yes, in East Finchley.'

Disdaining surreptitiousness, he reached out and picked up her left hand. 'And do you live alone?'

'No, I don't.'

'Ah.'

The note of disappointment in his voice made Ginny give a wicked grin. 'I live with—another girl.'

'Do you, indeed?' His face brightened.

'Could you fasten your seatbelts, please? We'll be landing very shortly.' The stewardess removed their cups and put up the tables.

Turning towards her, this intriguing stranger said, 'This flight has been much, much too short.' Then, persuasively, 'Look, I have a two-hour wait for my connection to Stockholm. Are you being met, or could you possibly stay and have a drink with me?' Ginny hesitated and he said, 'It would give us a chance to get to know each other better, and then you might not refuse me if I asked you for a date.'

She was supposed to contact the shoot as soon as she arrived, but Ginny looked at his leanly handsome face and knew that, as much as she wanted to make a good impression with the crew, this was a chance not to be lightly thrown away. 'All right,' she agreed. 'But only for a short time, I'm afraid. I'm supposed to start work this afternoon.'

'That's great.' He gave her a smile that made her feel suddenly breathless.

Ginny turned away, feeling slightly stunned, and picked up her handbag to grope for a handkerchief. Her initials, V.B., in gilt letters, were attached to the lower corner of the bag. But then they started to land so she dropped the bag back on the floor and turned to her neighbour with expressive eyes. He grinned and took hold of her hand.

When they landed he helped her into her coat and Ginny put on her hat and gloves, then they were quickly disembarked before the rest of the passengers. As they walked along the long corridor there were notices instructing passengers connecting with another flight to take a different route. Glancing at them, he said, 'It looks as if I'll have to leave you here for a while.'

'How will I find you?'

'Don't worry. I'll meet you the other side of Customs. Just wait there till I come.'

'All right.' She gave him a happy, dazzling smile. 'See you shortly.'

Lifting a hand in acknowledgement and farewell, he turned and walked briskly down the other corridor. Ginny looked at his broad back in the dark overcoat for a moment before she, too, turned and hurried to go through Passport Control and collect her cases. A great inner excitement filled her, and a deep-down intuition that maybe something fantastic was going to happen. She had set out for Paris hoping that the modelling assignment might change her life, but now there was also the almost fearful possibility that it might change in another way, too. It was such a thrilling discovery that it wasn't until Ginny was standing waiting for her cases to appear on the carousel that it suddenly occurred to her that she didn't know his name. The journey had been so short and the transition from being complete strangers so swift that they just hadn't got round to exchanging names. The thought made her laugh aloud, and a woman standing next to her turned and said, *'Comment, mademoiselle?'*

'C'est rien.' But the smile stayed on her face as Ginny thought that a man had picked her up without even asking her name.

Her cases came through and she lifted them on to a trolley and went through Customs without difficulty. The concourse outside was crowded and she couldn't see her flight companion, but that was hardly surprising as she'd got through so quickly. Pushing her trolley out of the way of the emerging passengers, Ginny moved to a quieter spot to wait.

She looked eagerly around her, not knowing from which direction he'd come, and amused herself by trying to guess what his Christian name would be. Not something terribly modern like Wayne or Scott, she decided; somehow they would be wrong for his character. He needed a name that showed strength and reliability, like Bruce. In Ginny's mind she felt that a scientist must have all the old-fashioned virtues. Glancing at her watch, she saw that almost ten minutes had gone by. Either he had got held up in Customs or he also had the scientist's fault of absent-mindedness, she thought with a smile.

As another ten minutes passed and he still didn't appear, Ginny's impatience began to change to annoyance and then anger. She wasn't used to being stood up and she certainly wasn't used to having childish tricks played on her. Again she looked round, indecisive about what to do. She'd never waited this long for any man before. A great feeling of bitter disappointment filled her. He had seemed so nice. And she had agreed to give up some of her precious time to know him better! Ginny looked at her watch again.

It was almost half an hour now. Making up her mind, she angrily pushed the trolley towards the exit doors, striding purposefully along and deliberately not looking back, so that she didn't see a man in airport uniform who came to search for her among the people standing around.

Taking a taxi to her hotel near the Boulevard Haussmann, Ginny checked in and was handed an envelope from the shoot organiser telling her where to meet the crew. Feeling guilty about the time she had wasted, she quickly dumped her cases in her room then took another taxi to the Place du Tertre in Montmartre to join them. The day was bright and dry but there was a cold wind that had made the café proprietors close all the gay parasols above the tables out on the pavements. Even so, there were still enough tourists tough enough to brave the wind and sit at the tables or to crowd round the artists who were *habitués* of the square.

Quite a few tourists were also gathered round the crew as they photographed one of the models with an arm thrown negligently across an artist's easel. Going up to them, Ginny waited until they'd finished the shot, then made herself known to the organiser. 'Hello, I'm Virginia Barclay.'

The woman turned to look at her. 'Oh, you're one of the twins.'

Ginny tried hard not to look rueful. It was to be expected, of course; she and Venetia had been trying to find work as a pair for too long not to be known, but it would have been nice, on this, her first assignment alone, to have been thought of as an individual. 'That's right. I'm called Ginny.'

The older woman nodded approvingly. 'Well, you're certainly what we were looking for. Are you ready to start work? How's your hair?' Ginny took off her hat and the woman looked at her hair critically. 'Oh, good, you've washed it this morning. You've no idea of the number of girls who don't.' She pointed to a nearby café. 'We've taken an upstairs room over the café to use as a changing-room. You'll find the dresser and make-up girl in there. Tell the dresser to put you in the lavender suit.'

From that moment on the afternoon was hectic but Ginny loved every minute of it. At first she was a little nervous but the photographer told her a really corny joke that made her laugh, and the other girls were friendly, so she was soon at ease. The photographer, Simon Blake, seemed to be pleased with her too, which helped a lot. They went on working until the light gave out, then changed into ordinary clothes and went downstairs to the café for a meal. Except for the photography and lighting side, they were all women on the shoot, none of whom Ginny had met before. She was by nature a little reserved; when you spent your whole life in the close company of a twin sister you didn't really need anyone else. But tonight, perhaps because of her disappointment over the man she'd met on the plane, Ginny felt a great need for companionship, so she more than met her colleagues halfway. She was eager to learn and to listen, too, and didn't put herself forward, so they soon accepted her as one of themselves.

'It must be weird having a twin sister,' one of the girls said to her. 'Are you identical twins?'

Ginny nodded a little wryly; it was a question she'd been asked thousands of time before. 'Yes, absolutely identical. No one can tell us apart.'

'No one? Not even your parents?'

'They used to be able to, but they split up some years ago and we lived with our mother. We see our father very occasionally and he can't tell us apart now.'

'But surely your mother must be able to?'

Ginny gave a mischievous grin, her eyes sparkling. 'My sister had a small mole on her neck and our mother always told us apart by that, but then Venetia had the mole removed and Mummy was completely fooled. She'd got so used to using that as a guide that she didn't know what else to look for. Now she goes by instinct mostly, although she says that our voices are just slightly different. But we've proved her wrong on that one, too, several times.'

'How about boyfriends?' she was asked by her avid listeners.

'Oh, they definitely can't tell the difference. In fact, we often swap dates without the boyfriends' realising.'

'And you really get away with it?'

'Of course.'

'But don't you give yourselves away? I mean, you can't both like the same men. What if your sister is willing to go further with a man than you are—he'd find it a bit odd if his date was passionate one night and frigid the next, wouldn't he?'

'We probably wouldn't swap if it was a guy one of us really liked. Usually we only do it with men we've just met so we can both give him the once-over; that way they don't know us too well and we don't get caught out.'

'And what happens when you've given them the once-over?' her listener asked, intrigued.

'Well, I'm afraid we usually pull them to pieces before we decide which, if either of us, is going to go out with him.'

'How do the men feel about that when they find out?'

'They don't, usually. If they don't already know that we're twins we often don't tell them. When you live in your sister's pocket all the time there has to be some part of your life that you don't share. But it's difficult because we not only live together but we also work together and have largely the same interests, so the people we meet tend to know about us anyway.'

'I'm amazed that you can get away with it,' the girl next to her said, shaking her head in fascination.

'But we've been taking each other's place ever since I can remember,' Ginny told her, and went on to describe how she and Venetia, as children, had used their identical appearance to fool various schoolteachers so that Ginny went to all the classes she enjoyed and vice-versa for Venetia. 'But they got wise to it eventually, and insisted on our wearing different-coloured blouses.'

'And did that work?'

Ginny laughed. 'Of course not. We just swapped blouses, so in the end they just made us both go to *all* the classes. Which was a fitting punishment as we both had to take subjects we hated.'

'How fantastic. I wish I had a twin sister; it must be marvellous,' one girl said on a strongly wistful note.

'Yes, it is,' Ginny agreed. But her eyes grew shadowed. Most of the time it was marvellous, of course, but there were times—and especially just lately—when she almost wished that her relationship with Venetia could be that of ordinary sisters. They had been brought up so closely, their mother dressing them alike and not allowing one of them to go anywhere without the other, that sometimes she felt as if they might as well be joined like Siamese twins. And because they were so close they were often on the same wavelength. Rather like an old married couple, they didn't even have to look at each other to know what the other was thinking. Sometimes they even answered each other without a question being asked.

Now it was completely automatic, as soon as she got back to the hotel, for Ginny to pick up the phone and call Venetia at their shared flat in North London. The call was answered almost immediately. Another knack they had was always knowing when the other was going to be in contact. Without bothering to ask who it was, Venetia, her voice a reverberation of Ginny's, said, 'Hi, how did it go?'

'Great. I'm really enjoying it. They're a very friendly crew.'

'Who's in it?'

Ginny named everyone in the crew and described the work they'd done that day in detail.

'It sounds fun,' Venetia said wistfully. 'I wish I were there.'

'I know. It would have been a really good day—except for one thing.'

'Tell me.'

It didn't occur to Ginny not to; she was so used to sharing everything with Venetia, even her disappointments—perhaps especially her successes and disappointments. 'I met a man on the plane. He was so nice; good-looking and easy to talk to. I—I liked him.'

'Don't tell me—he made a clumsy pass at you.'

'No, it wasn't that. He had a couple of hours between flights in Paris and he asked me to have a drink
with him, that was all. But we had to split up to go
through Customs and he didn't show up.'

'Perhaps there was a reason,' Venetia said
comfortingly. 'Who was he?'

'A scientist. A physicist in the physics department
of a university.'

'That all sounds very impressive, darling, but I
meant what was his name?'

'I don't know,' Ginny confessed. 'We didn't get as
far as exchanging names.'

'But you agreed to meet him for a drink,' Venetia
pointed out in amusement.

'So that I could get to know him well enough to
find out who he was. You just don't blurt out your
name to some stranger who happens to sit next to you
on a flight. That would be stupid.'

'It was even more stupid to lose him if he was that
dishy,' her twin pointed out with demoralising logic.
'What university does he work at?'

'He didn't get round to telling me that either,' Ginny
admitted. 'Unfortunately it was a very short flight.
All I really know is that he was on the way to
Stockholm to read a paper at a scientific conference.'

Venetia was silent for a moment, taking it in, then
said, 'You're quite sure you weren't having halluci-
nations or something? Perhaps you were light-headed
from lack of oxygen. Because he definitely doesn't
sound at all dishy to me, rather dull in fact.'

'*You* didn't see him,' Ginny pointed out. 'He was...'
she remembered his own words about her and smiled
'...a refreshing change.'

'Well, that doesn't sound as if you've gone completely overboard about him. You haven't, have you?'

'No, of course not,' Ginny said firmly, determinedly trying to stifle the sharp disappointment, to forget that singing excitement that he'd made her feel. 'I'm just annoyed that he stood me up, that's all.'

'Forget about him,' Venetia counselled. 'Where are you going to shoot tomorrow?'

'Along the Seine,' Ginny replied, deliberately putting enthusiasm back into her voice and pushing her hurt feelings to the back of her mind.

But when she lay in bed that night, unable to sleep in the strange surroundings and missing Venetia more than she could have thought possible, Ginny's thoughts went back to the man on the plane. She just couldn't imagine why he hadn't shown up. There had been something about him that had instantly attracted her and she was willing to swear that he had felt the same. Perhaps, though, he was married, in which case he might have had second thoughts about meeting her again after he'd left her at the airport. If that was the case, Ginny was glad, because there was no way she wanted to get mixed up with a married man. It had happened to her, inadvertently, once before, when she'd been going out with a man for about three months before she found out he was married. By that time they had grown quite close and she had begun to listen to his urgent pleas to have an affair. But when she had found out that he was married she had dropped him immediately, angry not only that he'd deceived her but also because she had believed his lies. Her hurt and anger had been felt as deeply by her twin as by herself and since then she and Venetia had been more circumspect in the men they went out with, steering well clear of any that weren't free and single.

She fell asleep at last and over the next week managed not to think of the stranger more than a few times a day. She tried not to, but when she noticed a tall figure in the crowd she would look more closely, her heart suddenly lifting eagerly, only to be disappointed when it turned out to be someone else. It was a far-fetched hope, of course; it was hardly likely that he would come to Paris to search the streets for a girl he had met for only an hour. But, even so, the hope didn't completely die until the Paris shoot was over and they moved on to Venice to spend another week working there.

Ginny would have liked to telephone Venetia every evening to talk, but the calls were expensive and they agreed to only call once a week or in emergency. When she had left London Venetia had said cheerfully in answer to her fears, 'Don't worry; after a few days you'll be so taken up by the new job and new people that you won't even miss me. I'll be the one who's lonely; in the flat by myself with no one to talk to or go around with.' But that wasn't so, Ginny found. She missed not being able to share everything with her twin, to talk over the new experiences, discuss the places she'd seen and share the excitement. Despite the friendliness of the crew she often felt very alone, and so couldn't enjoy herself as much as she should have done. She supposed it was like being part of a close married couple—if one of them went away alone they would miss the other so much that they just longed to go home. But married couples, however long they had been together, had had some experience in the past of being individuals, whereas she and Venetia had not; they had been like a joined couple from the moment they were born.

Her big consolation during those weeks was that the photographer and organiser of the shoot were very pleased with her work. 'You're a natural,' Simon Blake told her. 'Look, give me the address of your agency. I've been asked to do several fashion assignments and I'll put in a word for you.'

'Why, thank you, that's marvellous.' Ginny glowed, but then felt a stab of guilt, and said, 'My twin, she's a model, too. And we're identical, so we could share any work.'

Simon gave her a strange look. 'I don't know how she photographs. Maybe she's as good as you. But it's hard enough in this business for one girl to get work, let alone two who're identical. I think you'll find that you're going to have to go your separate ways if one of you wants to succeed as a model.'

Ginny gave him an uncertain smile, feeling even more guilty, and when she rang Venetia that weekend she didn't pass on what the photographer had said. Instead she rather hesitantly gave the news that the girl she was replacing wasn't yet well enough to come back so the crew organiser wanted Ginny to stay on for another ten days or so while they went on to Florence and Milan.

But she needn't have worried. 'That's marvellous,' Venetia said at once. 'You must make the most of your chance.'

'I feel terrible about your not being here, sharing it with me.'

'That's silly. You won the toss, remember?'

'So I did. Anyway, what have you been up to? Are you OK? You've been on my mind a lot lately.'

'Have I?' Venetia gave an odd kind of laugh. 'I managed to get a few days' work as a mum-to-be, modelling maternity clothes. I had to tie a big pad round my waist to make me look pregnant. And just think how we starve ourselves to try to keep slim.'

Ginny laughed. 'I can't imagine you as pregnant. How about your social life; are you still going out with Dave?'

To her surprise there was a slight withdrawal in Venetia's voice as she said, 'Oh, no, I got bored with him.'

'There's no one else on the scene, then?'

'Not really.' Again there was a reserved note in her twin's voice, so slight that only someone who knew her as well as Ginny did would have noticed it. Intrigued, Ginny was going to question her further, but Venetia quickly changed the subject by saying, 'A letter came for you. Would you like me to read it to you?'

Instantly diverted, Ginny said, 'You're sure it's for me?'

'Yes, it has your full name on it, not just the initial.'

'OK. Better make it quick, though; this call must be costing a bomb.'

Venetia went to get the letter and the stupid hope that the man on the plane might have somehow traced her and written to her filled Ginny's heart. But the letter only turned out to be from a sports club that she'd applied to for membership.

The sisters didn't speak to each other again until the following weekend when Ginny was able to tell Venetia the time of her flight home.

'OK, I'll meet you at the airport,' Venetia replied. 'Look, darling, I'm sorry but I have to rush. I'm late already.'

'Got a heavy date?' Ginny asked laughingly.

But Venetia just said, 'Must go. See you next week. Take care.' And put the phone down.

A little piqued, Ginny put her receiver down too, but then forgot all about it as she went with the crew to have dinner at a nearby *trattoria* and had one of the best evenings of the whole shoot.

Florence was a breathtakingly wonderful city and they all crammed as much sightseeing into their time there as they possibly could before moving on to Milan to take the last shots. Taking British fashions to Milan was almost like taking coals to Newcastle, and to get its own back the rain poured down and it was very cold for the first three days they were in the city, so that they weren't able to work. They had to change flights and Ginny had to send a telex message to pass on to Venetia because, although she called nearly every evening, her sister was never in.

But she was there, waiting, when Ginny finally came through into the concourse at Heathrow. They waved, rushed to meet each other, and hugged tightly.

'Lord, how I've missed you!' They both said it together, then laughed delightedly.

'You've got more luggage,' Venetia exclaimed as she took over the trolley.

'Well, I did see one or two things in Italy that I thought we would like. And we were allowed to keep some of the clothes we modelled.'

'I can't wait to see them, and to hear all about it. Come on, I've left the car just outside.'

Their car was a beaten-up old Ford, so that it didn't matter too much if it got vandalised by being left on the street outside the flat all the time, and anyway they couldn't afford anything better.

Ginny wasn't at all surprised to find that the car was parked with one wheel up on the kerb and the back sticking out. Venetia was a hopeless driver. Automatically going round to the right-hand door, Ginny got in the driver's seat, and talked non-stop about the shoot the whole way home. Venetia sat quietly listening to her, and it was only when they got home that Ginny rather belatedly overcame her own high to realise that her sister might be feeling jealous. 'Sorry, you should have told me to shut up,' she apologised.

'No, I was fascinated.'

'But when you've been bored here at home alone...'

Venetia seemed to take a deep breath. 'Actually I haven't been all that bored. I've—I've met someone.'

'So that's why you were out every time I rang. Good, I'm glad you had someone to take you out. I've been feeling really guilty about having such a great time when you weren't.' She waited, but when Venetia didn't speak, said, 'Well, come on. Give. Who is he? Did you meet him since I've been away?'

'Well, yes.'

'So I don't know him, then. What's his name?'

Venetia hesitated. 'His name is Alex Warwick,' she said slowly. Adding, 'As a matter of fact you do know him—he's the man you sat next to on your flight to Paris.'

CHAPTER TWO

FOR a moment Ginny couldn't take it in. '*What* did you say?' Then she laughed. 'Hey, don't joke. Who is he, really?' But Venetia didn't answer and Ginny said slowly, reluctantly, 'You're not joking.' She shook her head disbelievingly. 'But I don't understand; how could you possibly have met him?'

'When he got back to England Alex wrote to every model agency in London, describing you, saying what little he'd learnt about you, that you lived in East Finchley. And he knew your initials; he'd glimpsed them on your handbag, so that helped.'

Ginny's eyes widened in thrilled excitement. 'He really did all that to try and find me?' But then she remembered what Venetia had said and the excitement faded. 'But he found you?' she said in disturbed puzzlement.

'Yes.' Venetia looked at Ginny and then away again as she went on, 'When the agency got Alex's letter they thought he meant me, you see, because of course they know my initials are V.B., but you're down on their books as Ginny instead of Virginia. So they phoned me and asked if I knew anything about a scientist who'd just got back from Stockholm, and of course I remembered what you'd told me so I said I did and they forwarded his letter to me.'

'And you opened it.'

'Yes. But then we always do open each other's letters when they're just addressed to Miss V. Barclay,

29

don't we?' Venetia said in a pleading tone, her eyes fixed on her twin's face. 'They could be for either of us.'

'But when you saw it was for me you still went ahead and read it.'

'I know I shouldn't have done, but I was so intrigued,' Venetia admitted. 'And, well, the letter just made me more curious. You see, Alex said that he would be coming up to London for a few days and would you meet him? Obviously I knew you couldn't make it so I thought I'd better go along to let him know that you'd been found.'

'You didn't tell me any of this on the phone,' Ginny said accusingly.

'No, because I wanted to make sure that I met him OK first. And...' She sighed and shrugged. 'I'm afraid I have to admit that curiosity got the better of me. I suppose I wanted to look him over, too.'

'And when you did?'

Going over to their drinks tray, Venetia poured out two stiff gins, handing one to Ginny. 'When I did he thought I was you, of course.'

Ginny looked into eyes an identical hazel to hers. 'And you didn't choose to enlighten him.'

Venetia shrugged. 'I was going to—but then I found out that you hadn't told him anything about me.'

She sounded a little hurt, making Ginny say defensively, 'He was someone I met on a plane; I wasn't about to tell him my life-story.'

'No, I suppose not.' Venetia's chin came up and she spoke rather defiantly. 'If I'd told him the truth he would never have believed me. You know no one does until they see us together. He would have thought that

I was making up a hare-brained story to try to get rid of him.'

'You could have shown him a photograph of us both,' Ginny pointed out tartly.

'Yes, I know. I thought of that afterwards, but by then—well, by then I found that I was interested in him myself.'

'Well, thanks very much,' Ginny exclaimed shortly. 'You knew I liked him.'

'No, I didn't. All you said about him was that you found him "a refreshing change". That didn't exactly sound as if you were over the moon about him. As far as I knew he was just someone you'd met that you'd found mildly interesting, that's all.'

It was true, Ginny realised; she had played down that wild feeling of excitement, an emotion so new that she hadn't wanted to share it even with the person closest to her. She bit her lip, but then said, 'And what about the way he felt about me? Didn't it occur to you that I must have really made an impression on him for him to go to the length of writing to every model agency in London to try and find me? Why, there must be dozens of agencies. Hundreds.'

Venetia gave her an unhappy look. 'That was mostly what intrigued me,' she confessed. 'I just *had* to see what he was like. You do understand, don't you? I'm—I'm sorry, Ginny.'

Ginny was silent for a moment, but then took a long swig of her drink and shrugged, trying to make the best of it. 'I suppose it was an irresistible temptation. OK, I'll forgive you.' Putting down the glass, she went over to the phone. 'Have you got his telephone number? I'll ring him—Alex—up now and tell him I'm home.' Alex, she thought, his name is Alex. It's exactly right for him.

'But he won't know who you are. He won't understand,' Venetia said unhappily.

'Won't know who I am? But you must have told him the truth by now, surely?'

'Well, no, I haven't actually,' Venetia admitted. Adding quickly, as Ginny swung round on her, 'Ginny, *I really like him*. I—I haven't felt this way about a man in ages. In fact I don't think I've ever felt this way about a man before.'

'But you hardly know him. You——' She broke off and looked hard at her sister. 'Just how many times have you seen him?'

'Quite a few. In fact, we've been going out together regularly since we met.'

'And what are his feelings about you?'

'I think he feels the same. Of course, it's early days yet, and——'

'But he still thinks you're the girl he met on the plane,' Ginny cut in.

Venetia nodded reluctantly. 'Yes.'

'And just how do you think he's going to feel about you when he finds out you're not?'

'Well, I wasn't actually planning on telling him.'

'*What?*' Ginny gave an amazed crack of laughter. 'You weren't going to tell him about me at all?'

'Oh, about you, yes. Of course. I just thought it would be nice if he could go on believing that it was me he'd met on the plane, that's all.'

'Oh, yes, that would be nice for you, wouldn't it?' Ginny said sarcastically. Then, in sudden bitter anger, 'But why the hell should I make it nice and easy for you? I met him first and *I* was the one that made such

an impression on him that he went to all that trouble
to find me.'

'Yes, I know,' Venetia said wretchedly. 'But——'

'But nothing,' Ginny cut in forcefully. 'I'm going
to tell him the truth.'

Her sister's face paled. 'Look, I can understand
your being angry, but you're not listening to me.
Ginny, I think—well, I think this might lead to something serious. I really care about Alex.'

'And just how the hell do you think I feel about
him?' Ginny shot back. 'I was so disappointed when
he didn't turn up. I kept thinking about him and hoped
desperately that he would try to get in touch with me.
And when he did you had to step in and take my
place.'

Venetia gazed at her in astonishment. 'I had no idea
you felt this way. You never told me. But you only
met Alex for an hour; your feelings for him can't
possibly be as strong as mine. I've been out with him
a dozen times at least, and we've started to develop
a relationship.'

'There was an instantaneous attraction between us,'
Ginny declared hotly.

Venetia stood still for a moment, staring at her, then
said hollowly, 'That's how I felt about him, too. Oh,
Ginny, don't say we've both fallen for the same man.'

Turning away, Ginny clasped her hands together to
try and stop them trembling. Overwhelmed by the
possibility that Venetia had brought out into the open,
she pushed it aside, afraid to face it. 'Did he—did
Alex say why he didn't meet me at the airport?'

Her voice unsteady too, Venetia replied, 'Yes, he
was terribly apologetic about that. It seems that because he was a transit passenger he wasn't allowed

through Customs. He tried to persuade the authorities there—even appealing to their French sense of romance—but they wouldn't let him through. All they would do was to take a message for him, but by the time someone went to look for you with it you'd already left.' Venetia hesitated. 'You obviously didn't wait very long. If Alex had made that much of an impression on you surely you could have waited until——'

'He knew I didn't have much time,' Ginny said shortly, turning round. 'I had to find the crew and join in the shoot that afternoon. I'd told him that I could only spare half an hour. And how was I to know that he couldn't get to meet me? I thought that perhaps he was married and had changed his mind or something.'

They were both silent for a long moment, until Ginny, hating to have to ask for the information, said stiffly, 'Is he married?'

'No. He never has been.'

'And what university does he work at?'

'Essex. That's why Alex is able to get down to London so easily.'

'I see.' Ginny turned away again, thinking how Venetia said his name with such easy familiarity. A great stab of jealousy filled her heart, an emotion she had seldom felt before and never with such intensity. And certainly never as far as Venetia was concerned. The closeness between them was so much deeper than any other emotion that they instinctively shied away from anything that would bring them into conflict, be it men, work, or anything else. They had a very occasional spat, of course, but usually it surprised them so much that they were laughing together over it the next minute. As well as feeling that her twin was the other half of herself, each thought of the other girl as her best friend and confidante. It hurt Ginny now to feel that Venetia had gone behind her back.

Working things out in her mind, she said, 'You deliberately didn't tell me that you'd met Alex so that you would have time to form this relationship, didn't you?'

'I suppose so,' Venetia admitted. 'The first time, though, it was as I said: I just went to meet him out of curiosity. But after that . . . Yes, I admit, I wanted him to like me.'

'And just what kind of relationship do you have with him now?'

'Quite close,' Venetia said reluctantly.

'Only *quite* close. Good heavens, you have been wasting your time,' Ginny said sarcastically, 'I should have thought you'd have him hooked by now.'

'Please, Ginny, don't be like this,' Venetia said in distress.

'How do you expect me to be, for heaven's sake?'

'Will you—will you tell him?'

'I don't see why I shouldn't. Anyway, I think he has a right to know.'

'I'd rather you didn't,' Venetia said tensely.

'And I'd rather you hadn't gone out with him,' Ginny snapped back.

They stood facing each other, two tall, slim, good-looking girls who suddenly found themselves at a crucial point in their lives. But because they were so close their first reaction was to back off, to try and defuse this strange and unpleasant atmosphere that had emerged between them.

'I'd better unpack,' Ginny said. 'Do you want to see the clothes I've brought back?'

'Yes, of course.'

They went into Ginny's bedroom and were both careful not to mention Alex again. Instead they talked about clothes and about the shoot, which helped a lot to dispel the antagonism between them.

'It sounds as if you did really well. I'm glad,' Venetia said sincerely.

At any other time Ginny would have felt a twinge of guilt at that, but now she recognised all sorts of underlying emotions in that simple remark. If she became busier as a model then Venetia would feel less guilty about Alex, and it also implied that her own ambitions to take up a modelling career had suddenly waned. She must be really serious about Alex, Ginny realised, which left her in a turmoil of emotions about what course of action to take. She ought, in the circumstances, to just bow out gracefully, she supposed. Especially if Alex was as smitten as Venetia seemed to be. But what if he wasn't and they broke up without Alex knowing that it was Ginny he had been attracted to first? They would both have lost him, then.

'I'm going to have a bath,' she said abruptly.

This was their way of saying that they wanted to be alone for a while; in the bathroom you could lock the door and have some time to yourself.

'Yes, of course.'

Venetia went to leave, but as she reached the door Ginny said shortly, 'When are you seeing Alex again?'

'Tonight, as a matter of fact.'

'Is he coming here to pick you up?'

'No, I'm meeting him in town; we're going out to dinner.'

'I want to meet him,' Ginny said abruptly.

'*Ginny!*'

'I don't know whether I'll tell him or not. I want to see how I feel when I meet him again. I'm not making any promises, but I'll see how I feel.'

'That's fair enough, I suppose.' But Venetia's eyes were unhappy.

'You needn't think I'll play gooseberry, if that's what you're afraid of,' Ginny said on a bitter note. 'I'll just have a drink and then leave you alone with him.'

'No, that's silly,' Venetia said at once. 'Of course you must stay and have dinner with us. I know that Alex will insist on it, too.'

'Well, we'll see how it goes.'

She went away, leaving Ginny free to lie in the bath and think how confidently Venetia had talked of herself and Alex as 'us' and how well she seemed to know him.

They each dressed separately for that evening, Ginny putting on a stunning black and white dress that she'd brought back from Italy, and drawing two wings of hair back from her face to form a plait at the back, leaving the rest loose. It was a style she didn't often use but she wasn't at all surprised, when they met in the sitting-room, to see that Venetia had chosen the same way of doing her hair and was also wearing a black dress. It happened to them all the time.

Venetia gave a wry laugh when she looked at Ginny. 'Alex is never going to believe that we didn't do it on purpose.'

'What have you told him about me?'

'Only that I have a twin sister.'

'Didn't you tell him about our modelling work or the nightclub act?' Ginny queried, referring to their stage act in which they sat on either side of a large frame and copied each other's actions as if it were a mirror image.

'I mentioned them, but I didn't go into detail,' Venetia admitted rather shortly.

'You didn't even tell him that we're identical, did you?' Ginny guessed.

Venetia shrugged and shook her head.

'You were wishing that I didn't exist, I suppose,' Ginny said with hurt in her voice.

'No, never that.' Venetia quickly put her hand on Ginny's arm. 'Don't ever say that,' she said forcefully. 'You know it isn't true. I'd give my life for you.'

Ginny touched her hand but said, 'Ah, your life, yes. But would you give up Alex?'

She said it flippantly, but there was a serious undercurrent in her tone. Venetia recognised it but merely said, 'Come on, kid sister. Let's go.'

They took a taxi up to central London, rather than drive around for ages looking for somewhere to park, but they got mixed up in a traffic jam of cars trying to get to a jazz concert and were held up anyway. In the end they abandoned the taxi and walked the rest of the way to the restaurant. Because of the delay they were a little late and Alex was already there. He was sitting on a stool in the bar area, a gin and tonic in front of him. Ginny would have known him anywhere. She went in ahead of Venetia and paused in the doorway, her eyes resting on him, taking in everything she remembered.

Alex got quickly to his feet when he saw her and strode over to take her hands. 'Hello.' He smiled into her eyes, his own proud, happy. 'You look beautiful tonight—but then you always do.' And he bent to kiss her.

It was only a brief kiss of greeting, but his lips were warm and possessive, sending an erotic surge of longing shooting through her. In just those few moments Ginny's heart felt as if it had swollen to fill her chest so that she could hardly breathe. She drank in his mouth in delight.

'Hi, remember me?' Venetia's voice sounded dimly in the background, breaking the spell.

Alex turned to look, then did a convulsive double-take, his mouth falling open. His eyes shot from one to the other of them. 'Good God! I'm seeing things.'

'Seeing double, actually.' Venetia smiled at him, at the same time giving Ginny an anxious look, fully aware of the effect that kiss had had on her. 'You remember I told you I had a twin sister? Well, this is her—she. My sister Ginny.' She stumbled nervously over the words, afraid of what Ginny might do and say.

'Good heavens!' Alex shook his head in disbelief, still looking at first Ginny and then Venetia, his eyes searching for some difference between them and finding none. 'But you're absolutely...' Completely taken aback, he groped for a word.

'Identical. Yes, we know,' Ginny said a little drily.

'I can't get over this. Sorry, I suppose you get this reaction all the time.' Then he realised the mistake he'd made and shook his head in rueful apology. 'I don't usually go up to strange women and kiss them.' Looking into Ginny's smiling eyes, he grinned in return. 'I suppose you play that trick all the time. You certainly had me completely fooled.'

Ginny looked at Venetia. 'Yes, we do, don't we?' she said with irony.

Venetia flushed a little but went up to Alex and put her arms round his neck to give him a more ardent kiss than he deserved. It was her way of saying to Ginny, Keep off, can't you see he's already mine?

Alex certainly enjoyed it, although he gave Venetia a quizzical look before glancing back at Ginny's set face. Then he said easily, 'Come and have a drink, both of you.'

He was full of questions, of course, all the usual ones, a few that weren't, and a lot that he couldn't ask. But all the time he was talking to them his eyes went from one face to another, still amazed and looking for some way of telling them apart. Venetia said Ginny's name often, so emphasising her own identity, and he knew which of them was which because their clothes were different. But he was visibly shaken, Ginny could see that. She supposed it must be quite a shock to fall for one girl only to find that she had an exact double. The three of them drew a lot of attention in the restaurant, too, the barman, unable to take his eyes off the girls, making a comment about Alex having twice as much luck as anybody else.

'I've told Ginny she's to stay and have dinner with us,' Venetia told Alex.

'Of course she must.' He smiled at Ginny warmly. 'I should like to hear all about you—although I feel as if I know you already.'

His eyes crinkled as he smiled at her, just the way she remembered from the plane. Her heart gave a little skip and she gazed back at him, trying to quell a feeling of loss and longing. Her lips parted to speak but Venetia said quickly, 'Here's the waiter with the

menus. I'm starving. Are you? What shall we have?'
She prattled on, her voice over-vivacious in her
eagerness to stop Ginny from speaking.

Slowly Ginny dragged her eyes from Alex's face and
met an imploring look from her twin. Biting her lip,
she looked away and picked up the menu. Venetia
needn't have brought her along and she certainly
needn't have asked her to stay for dinner; the least
Ginny could do was to hold back for tonight. Thinking
this, she looked at Venetia and her sister nodded,
reading the unspoken reassurance. A look of relief
came into Venetia's eyes and she turned to make some
laughing remark to Alex, at ease again.

It was a strange kind of meal, both exciting and
distressful. Ginny was eager to know more about Alex
and enjoyed talking to him and finding out about him.
He lived in Colchester, he told her, not far away from
the red-brick university of Essex where he lectured,
sharing a house with two other single lecturers. He'd
been at the university for two years, having spent some
time in industry after taking his D.Phil.

'D.Phil?' Ginny queried.

'Doctor of Philosophy.'

'I though that was a PhD.'

'It's the same thing. It just has different initials if
you took it at certain universities including Oxford or
Cambridge.'

'Which did you go to?'

'Cambridge.'

He must be really brainy then, Ginny realised,
feeling strangely pleased. Doctor Alexander Warwick.
It sounded good. She smiled at him. 'How did your
trip to Stockholm go?' she asked without thinking.

'Was your paper duly discussed? It was on the use of laser materials in industry, wasn't it?'

Alex's eyebrows rose and Ginny felt a sharp kick from Venetia under the table. 'Yes, that's right. I see your sister has been talking about me.' He threw a smiling look at Venetia. 'But I'm surprised you remember; I don't think I've mentioned it since that time we talked on the plane.'

'Probably I told Ginny about it when I spoke to her on the phone at the time,' Venetia said faintly.

'Really?' His smile broadened and he reached out to cover her hand with his. 'I didn't think I'd made that much of an impression.'

Venetia flushed and glanced away from Ginny's angry look. 'Don't get big-headed about it,' she said lightly. 'We always tell each other everything.'

'Everything?' Alex asked in half-serious alarm, his eyebrows rising.

'No, not quite everything,' Ginny put in. 'At least, not lately. Do we, Venetia?' she added meaningfully.

'Well, that's a relief,' Alex said with a laugh. He looked from one to the other of them and perhaps caught the undercurrent of tension. 'Let's have another bottle of wine.'

He enjoyed the rest of the evening; he could hardly help it with both girls vying with each other to entertain him. It was something they had done before a few times when they had both been taken out by one man, usually their agent or a mutual friend. They were both bright, intelligent girls with sparkling wit, and they enjoyed making a game of competing for the man's attention. Their conversation was animated and sparky and there wasn't a man alive who wouldn't have revelled in their joint attention. Alex was no exception, looking from one to the other of them as they kept him laughing and amused. Ginny wasn't sure which one of them he had looked at most; she thought perhaps she had the edge but maybe it was a tie.

At eleven-thirty the restaurant was almost empty and Alex looked reluctantly at his watch. 'I'm afraid we'll have to go. I've got lectures to give tomorrow.'

He helped them both into their coats and they waited in the entrance while Alex went to get his car. They were both silent, going over the evening, re-alising that what had been a game before had been much more serious tonight. Ginny would have charmed him away from Venetia if she had been able to; they both knew it. When Alex brought his car round Venetia went firmly round to the passenger door to sit beside him and Ginny had to sit in the back. It made her feel like a gooseberry, which angered her, especially when she thought that it ought by rights to be she who was sitting beside him.

He was a good driver—and he already knew his way to East Finchley, Ginny realised with another stab of jealousy as Alex drove confidently through the now quieter streets. When they'd cleared central London and were heading for the suburbs, Alex glanced at Venetia. 'When am I going to see you? How about this weekend?'

'We're booked to take part in a cabaret on Saturday,' Venetia answered with regret. 'But I'm free on Sunday.'

'Why don't you come and watch our act?' Ginny put in impulsively. 'We're performing as part of the entertainment for a company dinner and dance in Hemel Hempstead. That wouldn't be too far for you to come, and they usually let us join in the dancing afterwards.' She leaned forward, putting her arms on the back of the front seats, and Alex gave a swift grin at her eager face.

'I'd enjoy that. I'd like to see your act. It must be most unusual.'

'Not really,' Venetia said in a suddenly tight voice. 'We've been doing it since we were kids. Our mother pushed us into going to stage school, you see. She has great ambitions for us.'

There was a slightly bitter note in her voice and to cover it Ginny said quickly, 'We can sing and dance, too. But then, so can nearly every other girl who wants to go on the stage. So we decided to make use of our only unusual asset and stick to the mirror act.'

'Which do you want to do most?' Alex asked. 'The stage or modelling?'

'Modelling,' Ginny said positively.

Alex turned to look at Venetia. 'And you?'

She gave a small shrug. 'The same, I suppose.'

'What do you mean, you suppose?' Ginny demanded. 'You were crazy on the idea the last time I saw you.'

'And you enjoyed the work you did in Paris,' Alex reminded her.

For a moment Ginny was taken aback and thought he was talking to her, but then realised that Venetia must have misled him about that as well; if she wanted Alex to believe that it had been her on the plane she would have had to lie about the modelling assignment too.

'*Did* you enjoy it, Venetia?' Ginny said with sugar-sweet sarcasm.

'As much as you enjoyed your trip to Italy,' Venetia returned, giving as good as she got.

Perhaps it was just as well that Alex pulled up outside the flat then. It was a first-floor flat and they had to share the front entrance. Alex walked to the door with them and Venetia unlocked it, then looked meaningfully at Ginny.

Holding out her hand, Ginny said, 'Goodnight, Alex. Thanks for tonight; it was fun.' He put his hand in hers to shake it but she leaned forward and kissed him lightly on the cheek. 'Don't keep this sister of mine too long, will you? She needs her beauty sleep.' And, with a sardonic glance at Venetia, Ginny went inside.

The other girl followed her in just a few minutes, but it was long enough for Ginny to start feeling jealous again. But when Venetia came in she was angry. 'You just had to make that last remark, didn't you? You've been picking on me all evening.'

'On the contrary, I thought I was very reticent in the circumstances. Just how many lies have you told him?'

'I didn't actually lie; he just assumed things that weren't true, that's all.'

'Huh!' Ginny retorted in disgust.

Venetia dropped her coat on to a chair. 'You liked him, didn't you?'

'I liked him the first time I met him—did you really think I wouldn't now?'

'No, I suppose not.' Venetia sighed. 'It was just a forlorn hope, that's all.' Ginny had thrown herself moodily into a chair and kicked off her shoes and Venetia did the same. She looked at her twin for a few moments, trying to decide what to do, then said pleadingly, 'You could see that he liked me, couldn't you?'

'I could see that he had gone on liking the girl he met on the plane—namely, me,' Ginny retorted.

'You're being extremely obstinate and petty,' Venetia said angrily.

'And you're being extremely untruthful and underhand.'

'Are you going to back down and give me some space with Alex?'

'Are you going to tell him the truth and let me take him over?' Ginny countered.

'No! *Never*.' Venetia said it so fiercely that Ginny stared at her, her lips parted in surprise.

'You have got it badly.'

'Yes, I suppose I have.' Venetia gazed down at her hands for a long moment before looking at Ginny with wide, vulnerable eyes. 'I've never felt this way about a man before.'

They stared at each other, realising that in this, as in so many things, they felt the same way. They sighed at the same time.

'So it looks like stalemate,' Ginny said.

'Yes, I suppose it does,' Venetia agreed reluctantly.

Tacitly, they dropped the subject and went into their bedrooms to undress, but met again in the kitchen when they went to get their bedtime drinks.

'I wish you hadn't invited Alex to watch our act,' Venetia said irritably.

'Why not? It's not that bad.'

'I know that; it's not the point.'

Ginny knew full well what she was getting at but chose to be obtuse. 'What is it, then?'

'When we do the act we dress exactly alike.'

'Naturally.'

Venetia rounded on her. 'Oh, don't be so infuriating. If Alex sees us like that, he'll be even more
aware of how identical we are, and it might just occur
to
him——'

'That *I* was the one he met originally. Yes, that
thought did cross my mind.'

'*Please* don't let him find out, Ginny.' Reaching out,
Venetia caught her arm. 'I don't often ask you for
anything, but I'm begging for this. Please leave us
alone.'

Ginny looked into her twin's eyes, then pulled her
arm away with a jerk. 'I don't know. I'm angry. I'm
upset. Alex—he *matters*. Hasn't it occurred to you
that my feelings for him are exactly the same as yours?
All right, this is the first time we've ever felt the same
over a man, but does that mean that one of us has
to back down? And, if so, why the hell should it be
me after you've played such an underhand trick to
get to know him?'

Venetia looked away, biting her lip. 'I'm sorry,
Ginny. I just didn't know it was going to work out
like this.'

But Ginny went on angrily, 'Seeing Alex again made
me remember everything I liked about him. I just
don't know what I'm going to do. I might make a
play for him, I might not. I feel torn between the two
of you and that makes me angry. I don't want to be
in this position—but you're the one who's put me in
it, Venetia.' Swinging petulantly away, Ginny said,
'Oh, for heaven's sake let's forget about it for tonight
and get some sleep. We ought to go round to the
agency in the morning and we'll look like hags.'

'We needn't both go. I'll go by myself and you can
have a lie-in.' She gave Ginny a sympathetic look. 'You
must be tired after your journey and—and all this.'

Ginny was about to agree when she remembered that Simon Blake, the photographer, had promised to try to get her on his future assignments. But he'd stipulated that he only wanted her. It was Ginny's turn to feel guilty. She hesitated, wondering whether to tell Venetia, but then decided not to. It might have been one of those false promises that people meant at the time but promptly forgot, so nothing might come of it, in which case she would have made Venetia feel jealous for nothing. But then the thought occurred to her that maybe Venetia wouldn't be jealous; maybe she'd be glad because it evened things out between them.

'No, I'd rather go myself. They'll want to know how the shoot went for me,' Ginny said abruptly. Then she yawned. 'But you're right, I am tired. Goodnight. I'll see you tomorrow.'

Alone in her room, Ginny lay in bed staring at the moonlit ceiling, thinking that a few weeks ago she wouldn't have dreamed of having a secret from her twin, they would have told each other everything. But now they had each begun to deceive the other, and all because of a chance meeting with a man on a plane. They had never really competed against one another before, either, always thinking of themselves as a team. But now Ginny realised that whatever came of this shared attraction to Alex things would never be quite the same again. Maybe it was natural, maybe they were coming to an end of being a pair and it was the right time for them to start going their own ways and become individuals. But they had been brought up so closely that she was almost frightened at the thought. It was a thing that should have happened to them very gradually, Ginny thought unhappily, giving them time to get used to the idea, not by this sudden feeling that the person closest to you in the world was also your rival—and almost an enemy.

The next day Ginny went along to the modelling agency to report on the shoot, and to her pleasure found that Simon Blake had already contacted the agency, praising her work and asking for her for a shoot in a couple of weeks' time. It was only for a two-day contract, but the fact that she'd been specially requested for it boosted Ginny's morale no end.

'And Simon Blake left a message for you,' the girl at the agency told her. 'Would you contact him at this number.'

'Oh, thanks.' Ginny took the message slip, wondering what Simon wanted.

Well, she had to thank him for getting her the assignment so she might as well phone him straight away. Using the agency's phone, she called the number. A girl answered. 'Simon Blake's studio.'

'Oh, hello. This is Ginny Barclay. Simon left a message with my agency asking me to call.'

'Just a moment, please.'

There was a short wait before Simon came to the phone. 'Hello, Ginny. Look, I'm rather busy just now. Can you come round to my studio about twelve-thirty and then go on for lunch?'

'Why, yes, of course. I wanted to——'

But, 'Good,' Simon interrupted. 'Do you know the address?'

'No.'

He gave it to her, Ginny hastily writing it down, then immediately rang off. She wasn't entirely surprised by his abruptness; he had been a bit that way on the shoot, but mostly when he was working, during the leisure hours he had been more sociable.

The studio was in Chelsea, so Ginny took a tube train to South Kensington station and walked the rest of the way. It was situated over the top of an office equipment shop and marked by a discreet sign on a door at the side. Ginny went through the door, up a flight of quite wide stairs and through another door on the right of the landing.

The morning's photo session was just ending. Ginny was allowed into the huge studio to watch and stood waiting quietly in the background. It was evidently some children's fashion photography for a magazine or mail-order catalogue because there were toddlers in trendy gear running all over the place. But Ginny noticed that Simon had used photographs of giant-sized furniture as a background, so that the fashion shots would come out as if seen through the eyes of a child. It was a clever idea, but then Simon was beginning to get the reputation of being a very innovative photographer.

Simon took the last shots, told his assistant to clear up, the mothers to collect their 'brats' and take them home, shrugged on his jacket, put a hand on Ginny's arm and led her out of the studio. In his late thirties, successful, and with nothing to prove, he was full of confidence. 'My God, I'm glad that's over,' he said fervently when they were outside. 'Never work with more than one child; it's bound to lead to hell. Come on, there's a decent wine-bar down the street.'

Ginny laughed and fell into step beside him. 'How about animals?'

'Those are even worse,' Simon said feelingly. 'The damn things never stand still when you want them to.'

The people in the wine-bar obviously knew Simon well. A table had been kept for him and a bottle of cold white wine appeared without his saying a word. He poured some into two glasses and picked up his to take a long draught. 'I needed that,' he said fervently.

Ginny watched him with a smile but wondered if this was an everyday occurrence. A bottle of wine a day was close to alcoholism. But there were tired lines around his eyes, making her wonder if he worked and played too hard. There was a touch of grey in his thick curly hair, too.

'What would you like to eat?' he asked her. 'They do a good lasagne here.'

'I'll stick to salad, thanks.'

Simon gave a short laugh. 'It's one good thing about taking out models; you can always be sure that it won't cost much because they're always watching their figures.'

'Thanks for putting in a good word for me at the agency. And for asking for me on that next assignment,' Ginny said sincerely.

He gave a small shrug. 'It isn't much, but they're letting me pick my own models so I was able to do it. But I looked through your portfolio while I was at the agency and I'm sure that if you don't change it you won't get much more work.' He gave her a straight look. 'You know why, don't you?'

Ginny nodded slowly. 'The photographs are nearly all with my twin.'

'That's right. What individual shots you have are good, but they need to be all of just you. You're good, Ginny, but, as I told you before, you're not going to get anywhere as a double-act.'

There was a Chianti bottle with a red candle stuck in it on the table; the melted wax from a hundred other candles had trickled down the neck and hardened. How many other conversations had taken place at this table in the soft candlelight? she wondered. And had they been pleasant or as disturbing as this one was turning out to be? Troubled by his bluntness, she said slowly, 'Being a twin, an identical twin, isn't like having an ordinary existence, not when you've been brought up to do everything together as we have. It would be very hard to tell my sister that I was going to go it alone.'

He didn't understand and didn't pretend to. 'Nevertheless, that's what you're going to have to do. It's your choice, and I advise you to make it as soon as possible.'

'But then only one of us could make a career out of modelling.'

'Yes, so get in first. You needn't feel any disloyalty, if that's what you're afraid of. You're good, and you deserve to get on.'

'I don't know,' Ginny said unhappily.

'Well, if you do decide to go it alone you'll need a new portfolio. The individual photographs in the one you have could be better anyway.'

'They're the best we could afford. It cost a bomb.'

'I could do it for you, if you like,' Simon offered gruffly.

Ginny gave him a startled look. Not only did he do magazine and fashion photography, Simon also did portraits, so good that he was able to charge really high fees. She couldn't help but wonder if this was why he had invited her out to lunch, and said stiffly,

'Thank you, but I'm afraid I couldn't possibly afford your fee.'

'Who's talking about payment? I'm *offering* to do them for you.'

Her head came up as she stared at him. 'Why?' she demanded baldly.

A gleam of amusement came into his eyes but their food came and Simon didn't speak until it had been served. 'Because I think you're a natural. I believe that you could really go places, and one day you'll be in a position to choose your own photographer—and I hope that if I help you now you'll choose me.'

Her meal forgotten, Ginny stared at him in disbelief. 'But there are lots of girls better looking than us—me.'

'Perhaps, but you're photogenic. You know what to do without my telling you, and you stand and move well. Your bones and your skin are good, too. And your hair is beautiful.'

'Thank you,' Ginny said faintly.

'They weren't compliments, they were facts. And you're not responsible for the way you look, it's pure chance,' Simon told her, bringing her down to earth. 'As it is you're not making the most of your chances. But a portfolio by me would be a help.'

'It certainly would. Thank you.'

'Does that mean you're going to take up my offer?'

Ginny paused, knowing there was a question she had to ask but not wanting to. 'Would this—would this be a strictly business arrangement?'

Simon's mouth thinned and he gave a short laugh. 'No strings, do you mean?'

Ginny nodded, her eyes on his face.

His own eyes swept over her and she remembered the gossip she'd heard about him when they were in Italy; that he was in the process of getting his second divorce. 'Would strings be acceptable?'

'Sorry, no,' she said firmly, her chin coming up and her eyes meeting his steadily.

'Then there won't be,' he said calmly, apparently not in the least put out. He gave her a keen look. 'You're not likely to go off and get married or anything in the near future, are you?'

Ginny shook her head. 'I don't have a steady relationship with anyone, if that's what you mean.' She paused. 'If I do decide to take up your offer, then I should like to pay you back as soon as I'm able.'

He shrugged. 'Suit yourself,' he said shortly.

Realising that she was being churlish, Ginny gave him a dazzling smile. 'I'm sorry, I'm not used to such generosity. It's really very kind of you and I appreciate your interest in me.'

Mollified, he nodded. 'Just let me know when you make up your mind and we'll arrange some photo sessions.'

They talked of other things during the rest of the meal and afterwards Simon left her to go back to his studio. Ginny turned to go home, realising that yet another decision that could alter both her own life and Venetia's had landed squarely in her lap.

CHAPTER THREE

THERE were three acts in the cabaret that Saturday night. Ginny and Venetia were in the middle, between a singer on his way down and a young stand-up comic and impersonator who did a lot of television work—with rumours of soon having his own show—who was definitely on the way up. The twins were there because of the novelty of their act. It was a huge ballroom with round tables of diners set on three sides and the stage on the fourth. There was also a balcony that ran round the room. The meal was finished now, the speeches and toasts over, the guests noisy and expansive, but ready to sit and be entertained before they got down to the serious business of dancing the night away.

The girls had a dressing-room to themselves and were ready in their costumes and stage make-up. They waited silently, both feeling a little tense, as they always did before a performance. But then someone knocked on the door and a stage-hand brought in two baskets of flowers.

'Oh, how lovely.' Venetia eagerly read the card on hers. 'They're from Alex.'

'So are mine.'

'Well, he couldn't give to one of us and not the other, could he?' Venetia said rather sharply.

'I wonder where he'll be sitting?'

'Maybe we'll be able to see.'

Leaving the dressing-room, they went backstage and peeped through the curtain. The stage was full of the dance band's equipment so the singer was doing his act down on the dance-floor, a microphone in his hand.

'Can you see Alex?' Venetia asked.

'No.' Ginny pressed her eye against the gap in the curtain, careful not to disturb it. 'Wait, isn't that him up in the balcony? Straight in front of us. He's with another man.'

'Oh, yes, so it is.' There was something odd about Venetia's voice. Ginny gave her a frowning look but Venetia said quickly, 'Do you think our curtain will be wide enough to do the act properly from the dance-floor? We usually do it on a stage.'

'Of course it is. We've done it like this often enough. Why should tonight be different?'

'The room is so wide, and people are sitting right down the sides.'

'Well, there's nothing we can do about that, so don't worry about it.' Ginny glanced up at the balcony again. 'I wonder who Alex is with. Perhaps one of the staff.'

Venetia looked again but didn't make any comment, instead saying over-anxiously, 'You're sure the frame went together all right?'

'Yes, of course. Stop worrying.'

But it was always like this before a performance; Venetia was the more anxious and Ginny had to conquer her own nerves to soothe and encourage her twin. But Venetia seemed especially uptight tonight. Ginny gave her another puzzled look but decided not to say anything until after their turn. They had played on the same bill as the singer before and went to wait

in the wings as they heard him go into his last song.
Then they carefully looked each other over for a last
time, making sure that their hair and clothes were
exactly alike. They were wearing boa-trimmed nég-
ligés in deep pink over sets of lacy black underwear.

The singer finished on a rather cracked long note,
went back to take his bow, and then the stage-hands
carried their life-sized ornate gold frame, with curtains attached to long poles on either side of it, on to
the floor. Ginny was the one who appeared on the far
side of the mirror and so had to sneak on in the cover
of the curtains and wait. A dressing-table and a stool
with clothes on it was also put in front of the curtains, giving the impression of a bedroom.

The act was introduced by the compère, and Venetia
ran on as their music started and did a few dance-
steps away from the frame, giving the audience the
impression that she was the solo performer in a dance
routine that involved a mirror. Then, exactly timed
to the music, she went to sit in front of the frame as
Ginny did the same from the rear, each facing the
other. They then did the same actions, starting with
the usual, easy things of combing their hair, pow-
dering their noses and spraying on perfume; the same
business that a dozen similar acts had done in the past.
But then they took the performance a stage further
as Venetia pushed aside the stool and slipped out of
the négligé, throwing it aside. She then began to dress,
putting on stockings, shoes, chunky costume jew-
ellery, and last of all a tight-fitting red velvet evening
dress with a slit up the side. And all the while of course
Ginny was doing the same but in reverse, every action
minutely timed. That part was easy because they could
see each other, but then Venetia began to dance,

moving away from the mirror, then past it and away again, with Ginny repeating the dance in mirror image on the other side. The beat of the music quickened as the girls whirled in time to it, and reached a crescendo with Venetia coming to a stop immediately in front of the mirror, arms outflung—then she turned away and Ginny jumped through the frame to stand beside her.

There was a great gasp from the audience, and then a storm of applause. Many of them had guessed, of course, but there were still a lot who had been convinced that it was a mirror. The twins went into their 'Sisters' routine to finish the act and ran off to applause sustained enough to call them back twice to acknowledge it.

Afterwards they were on a high, the adrenalin bubbling as they ran backstage. They were both laughing with relief that it was successfully over and pleasure that it had been so well-received. 'They really liked us,' Venetia exclaimed happily.

'Of course they did. What else did you expect? We were good.'

They hugged each other exuberantly, then stood back as the comic came up, ready to run on stage as soon as the girls' props had been cleared off. 'Break a leg,' they said in unison. He grinned at them but was almost as tense as they had been. Perhaps he needed to be when he had to hold the audience for the next half-hour. Going back to their dressing-room, the girls, hot and thirsty, opened a couple of bottles of ice-cold mineral water and drank them down.

'Shall we leave packing the props away until after the dance or do it first?' Ginny asked, coming reluctantly down to realities.

But Venetia was examining the black stocking covering her long and shapely right leg. 'Blow, I've laddered it. I thought I felt it go as I was putting it on.'

'Never mind, we can afford another pair. What with my modelling assignment money and the fee for tonight, we should be able to keep the wolf from the door for another couple of months at least.'

Venetia only murmured in answer, and Ginny, looking at her back as she continued to examine the stocking, realised that she was waiting for something. And it didn't take much guessing what for. Almost on cue there was a knock on the door.

Ginny turned to go and open it but Venetia called out, 'Come in,' so that as Alex walked in he got a good view of her legs.

'Girls, you were fantastic.' He came in, beaming with pleasure, then stood in the middle of the room looking at them before throwing out his arms in a surrendering gesture. 'OK, I give up; which one of you is which?'

Venetia laughed, ran to him, and put her hands on his shoulders. 'Will this help?' And she kissed him with sudden fierceness.

'Mm, definitely.' He smiled down at her, his arm round her waist. 'Congratulations, you were great.' Then he held out a hand to Ginny. 'You too, of course.'

Slowly Ginny went forward and put her hand in his. 'Thank you for the flowers.'

'It was my pleasure.'

'They're beautiful,' Venetia added. 'But you shouldn't have; you're spoiling me—us.'

'Nonsense. And I enjoyed your act immensely. You almost had me fooled, even though I knew what you were doing.' The girls glowed with his praise and Ginny left her hand in his, but Alex gently disengaged himself as he touched Venetia's arm. 'I wasn't the only one you fooled. I've brought a friend up with me. One of the other lecturers I share a house with.' He looked at Ginny, expecting her to be pleased. 'Can I ask him in?'

Much of the glow left Ginny's face and she looked quickly at Venetia, but her twin wouldn't meet her eyes.

'Yes, of course,' Venetia said for her. 'You haven't left him out in the corridor, have you? Bring him in at once.'

Alex hadn't shut the door properly. He went and pulled it open. 'Come in, Jeff—they're entirely decent.' And stood back as a man of about his own age and about the same height but much thinner, as if he was still a gangling sixth-former, walked into the room. His hair was thick and dark blond, falling on to his forehead, and he wore glasses, which he pushed back on his nose in a nervous gesture as Alex introduced him. 'This is Jeff Ferguson. Jeff, this is Venetia,' he paused as they shook hands, 'and this is Ginny.'

'Short for Virginia,' Ginny said clearly, emphasising the name and hoping that it would make Alex think. She was furiously angry. She didn't even have to look at her twin to know that Venetia had set this up. They *never* went out on blind dates. It was a pact they'd made years ago, when they were about seventeen and had been on several such dates, none of which had been enjoyable. And somehow they both found the whole idea of going out with a total stranger, chosen for them by someone else, and having to be nice to him because he was spending money on you, completely distasteful. And it was especially infuriating to know that Venetia had broken the rule just so that she could have a clearer field with Alex.

'I hope you didn't mind my coming along,' Jeff was saying as he shook her hand.

His grip belied his looks, being firm and strong, and Ginny looked up into a pair of shrewd brown eyes, their pupils magnified by the glasses. Trying to hide her own anger but not attempting to quell it, she said stiltedly, 'Of course not. I hope you enjoyed the cabaret.'

'It was incredible. The two of you are incredible. No wonder Alex said he can't tell you apart.'

Which brought them back to the usual mundane comment. Realising it, Alex said, 'The management have given us a table on the balcony. Shall we go up there and catch the end of the comedian's act?'

'We've got to change and get this stage make-up off first,' Ginny said at once, her eyes holding Venetia's. She wanted a word or three alone with Venetia.

But her twin took the cowardly way out, saying, 'I'd rather catch his act. We'll see you later, then.' Linking arms with Alex and Jeff, she smiled at them both and let them escort her out of the dressing-room.

Ginny scowled as the door shut behind them. The dresses they were wearing had cost a lot of money and they always made a point of changing out of them immediately after their performance. If anything got spilt on them it would cost a bomb to have them cleaned. Because of this they had brought other clothes to change into for the dance. Sitting down at the mirror and creaming her face, Ginny thought that Venetia had been acting out of character ever since she'd got back from Italy. No, even before that, when they'd talked on the phone and she hadn't told Ginny about meeting Alex. She had lied and cheated and now she was trying to palm Ginny off on some Peter Pan university lecturer.

Feeling very angry and ill-used, Ginny finished cleaning her face and added ordinary make-up, but didn't rush it, wanting to look good. The theatrical make-up, although fine under the harsh stage lights, wasn't flattering to their delicate bone-structure and colouring in dim or ordinary lighting. She went to change into the dress she'd brought with her, but then hesitated; Venetia would be expecting her to do that and would be glad because the men would more easily tell them apart. So, feeling bolshie, Ginny kept on the red velvet number and left her hair in the same style. By now her surface anger had subsided a little, but she still felt hurt by her twin's deviousness. Did Venetia really think that she was going to forget all about Alex just because he'd brought along a friend? If she'd wanted an escort she could have invited along any one of half a dozen men that she knew.

Going over to the baskets of flowers Ginny looked at the cards. Venetia's read, 'To Venetia. Good luck. Love, Alex.' But hers read, 'To Ginny. Good luck. Regards, Alex.' Did that mean that he was already in love with her sister? And she with him? Venetia was certainly behaving very oddly. But they had only known each other for a few weeks. OK, so Venetia might have felt the same instantaneous attraction that she had felt for Alex, but surely they weren't in love, not yet, not so soon?

It was an unpleasant thought that Ginny pushed aside, not wanting to believe it possible. Checking her appearance in the long mirror, for almost the first time in her life Ginny wished that she and Venetia weren't identical, that there had been some feature in herself that Alex would have remembered so that he would have waited for her and not gone out with her twin. But there was nothing. With a sigh, Ginny left the dressing-room and made her way up to the balcony where the others were waiting.

On the way she passed several people who stopped her to congratulate her on their act, which was always pleasant, so Ginny was smiling as she reached the balcony. Only Alex was there. Ginny's heart fluttered a little, amazed that Venetia had left him alone. He stood up as she came over.

'Venetia and Jeff are dancing. Let me get you a drink. What would you like?'

'Gin and tonic, please.' She held out a hand to stop him as he went to get it. 'But later will do. Why don't we dance first?'

'Of course. Great idea.'

As they went down the stairs to the main level Alex put a familiar arm round her waist, then drew back with a laugh. 'Sorry, I keep forgetting that you're not Venetia. I feel that I ought to know you as well as I know her, but of course we've only met once before.'

They reached the dance-floor and Ginny moved into his arms, glad that it was a slow number and they could dance close. He was just the right height for her, his shoulder just a few inches higher than hers, her eyes level with his mouth. It was a very sexy mouth, the top lip thin and straight, the lower one fuller, indicating a passionate temperament. Was he passionate? she wondered. Was that why Venetia was so crazy to keep him?

Testing him, Ginny said, 'Can't you feel any—shall we say emotional—difference between us? Are your feelings the same when you see me as they are when you see Venetia?'

Alex laughed. 'Mostly I feel hopelessly confused. Especially tonight when you're both dressed exactly alike. But I'm sure it will be easy to tell you apart when I get to know you both better.'

'I doubt it,' Ginny said rather shortly. 'Even our mother has difficulty.'

'I didn't mean by appearance; I meant by personality and temperament.'

She gave him a quick look, and took advantage of their almost knocking against another couple to put her hand on his shoulder and move slightly closer. He was wearing a musky, masculine aftershave that turned her on, made her want him to kiss her again. Stifling desire, she said, 'Maybe our personalities are identical, too.'

'Impossible,' Alex said with a definite shake of his head. 'No two people could be exactly alike.'

'Not even the way we've been brought up?' Looking into his eyes, Ginny's heart seemed to swell and she said in a tight voice, 'Our likes and dislikes are almost the same—we even like the same people.'

'You do?' His eyes flicked to her face, then rested there for a moment as she deliberately held his glance. But then he looked away as he said, 'That's hardly surprising, though. Most of us are drawn to people who're similar in outlook to ourselves, so as you and

Venetia are so alike you're bound to go for the same people.'

'But you've just said that no two people are exactly alike,' Ginny pointed out with a mischievous grin.

Alex laughed delightedly. 'Caught by my own generalisation! But in a way I think you've also proved my point, because I think you just have the edge on Venetia when it comes to wit.'

'Do I?' It was a compliment that didn't please her. 'You must think you know Venetia very well if you can make that judgement.'

He gave her an assessing look. 'Don't you like the idea of my getting to know her well?'

Ginny looked away, wondering how to answer such a forthright question. She certainly couldn't give a truthful one and say, No, because I want you to get to know me instead. But she didn't want to leave him with the impression that she was jealous of his friendship with Venetia either. Caught between the two she prevaricated by saying, 'What gives you that idea?'

'As you said, you've been brought up to be very close.'

Defensively, Ginny said, 'Venetia has had lots of boyfriends before.'

'I expect you both have.'

There was a slight note of reproof in his voice that annoyed her, but when Ginny looked up into Alex's face the anger died and her heart filled with frustrated longing. Can't you tell? she thought fiercely. Can't you see that it was me on the plane? That I was the one you went to all those lengths to meet again? Her heart began to thud. Why shouldn't she tell him the truth? He had a right to know, and she hadn't made any firm promise to Venetia. Licking lips sud-

denly gone dry, Ginny opened her mouth to speak—
but broke off abruptly as someone pulled at her arm.

'Hello, you two.'

It was Venetia, of course. Her twin gave her a fiery
look and Ginny realised that even across a crowded
dance-floor Venetia had picked up the danger signals
and had come rushing over. Jeff was behind her,
looking rather bemused, as well he might; Venetia had
probably been completely ignoring him ever since Alex
and Ginny had started dancing.

'Guess what?' Venetia said brightly. 'I've met three
people who've said they might be interested in using
us at other functions. Ginny, did we bring any of our
business cards along? We could give some of them
out.'

'I have some in my bag.' Ginny turned away to go
on dancing, but a passing couple paused to congratulate them on their act and by the time she'd politely
thanked them the music had come to an end.

Alex smiled down at her, said, 'Thanks, Ginny,'
and let her go, turning to wait for Venetia and Jeff
to come up to them. They all three moved off the
floor but Ginny paused for a moment before following them, feeling suddenly bereft, her arms empty.
It had been such a short dance, such a few moments
to be held close to the man she was so attracted to.
Such a short time in which to know for certain that
this was far more than just attraction.

As they reached the edge of the floor Jeff became
aware that she wasn't with them and turned to look
for her. He surprised the look of self-knowledge in
her face, her eyes, wide and vulnerable, fixed on
Alex's back. Jeff frowned in perplexity, but then his

brow slowly cleared and he come back and took her arm. 'You look as if you could do with a drink.'

'Yes. Please.' But then she hung back. 'But I . . .'

'There's a bar downstairs,' he told her, guessing her thoughts.

The bar was outside the dance hall, in a quiet spot where the music could hardly be heard, but there were several men in evening suits propping up the bar, talking shop, man-talk, their laughter loud and laced with drink. But Jeff led Ginny over to a table tucked away in a corner and screened from the bar by a couple of tall pot plants.

'You look like a Barcardi person to me,' Jeff said.

She smiled faintly. 'I'd rather have a stiff gin right now, but I'm driving so perhaps you could make it something long and not too alcoholic?'

'OK. Be right back.'

Ginny sat on the seat and felt as if she wanted to both laugh and cry at the same time. This ought to be the happiest moment of her life, discovering that she was in love, but her twin felt the same way and had stolen the man she wanted.

Jeff brought the drinks and sat down beside her. Ginny took a long pull of hers, feeling the ice-cold liquid hitting the back of her throat. 'What is it?'

'A Pimms without the fruit shop. I didn't think you'd go for that.'

Ginny nodded. 'Thanks.' She sat back in her seat, falling silent, her thoughts upstairs with Alex and Venetia.

'Would you like to talk about it?' Jeff asked after a while.

She turned to look at him, and read the compassion in his brown eyes. 'I don't need to, do I?'

'No, I suppose not. It's—unfortunate.'

Her lips twisting into a sardonic smile, Ginny said, 'Yes, I suppose you could say that.'

'Sorry.' Jeff pushed his glasses back up his nose. 'I suppose I'm not being very helpful.'

'Why should you be? You don't even know me. You certainly don't owe me anything.'

'You're a fellow human being and you're unhappy; if I can help I will,' Jeff said firmly.

'How can you possibly help?' Ginny said bitterly. And then, feeling that she'd given too much away to a stranger, 'And anyway I don't need any help. I'm perfectly OK.' Taking another swallow of her drink, she determinedly changed the subject. 'Are you a lecturer in physics, too?'

'No, in medieval history and archaeology.'

'Really? How interesting,' Ginny said politely.

Jeff laughed. 'Possibly. But not to you at the moment. Finish your drink and let's go and dance.'

So there was strength behind his mild exterior. Ginny meekly obeyed him and let him lead her out on the floor. The band was playing a fast number now and Jeff swung her into it. He could jive, too, although he seemed to be all arms and legs. Strangely Ginny enjoyed that dance, the fast beat temporarily driving out unhappiness as she whirled to the music. Even seeing that Alex and Venetia were dancing close by couldn't put her down completely. The sisters were both extremely good dancers, having been trained from an early age. They could follow a beat and were used to adapting their steps and style to a variety of partners so had no difficulty in following. People stopped dancing themselves to watch, and others came to the edge of the dance-floor, so that there was a spontaneous burst of applause when the music stopped.

Alex was flushed and laughing as he came over to them with Venetia. 'Good grief!' he exclaimed. 'That's the first time I've ever performed a floor show.'

'Stick with us, kid. You haven't even started to live yet,' Venetia retorted. She was clinging to his arm and laughing, too, her eyes brilliant with happiness.

Looking at her twin, Ginny was filled with such a mixture of emotions, of jealousy and self-contempt, of anger and sisterly love, that she had to turn abruptly away so that they wouldn't see. 'Excuse me.'

She hurried to the ladies' room and shut herself in a cubicle, leaning her head against the coolness of the tiled wall. This was crazy; she had to get control of herself. But her hands were shaking and it was hard to think straight. I must let Alex go, she told herself. I must put him out of my mind for Venetia's sake. I love her more than anything in the world and I mustn't spoil things for her now. I'll go away. I'll go to France and try and get work there. Or even America; they always need models in New York. She straightened up, trying to hang on to the resolve, but a picture of Alex smiling down at her filled her mind and she knew that she didn't have the strength to just give him up. Not yet. Not without a fight. She had the right to try and win him for herself.

When she came out of the cubicle Venetia was waiting for her and searched her face anxiously. 'Are you OK?'

'Yes, of course.' Ginny managed a smile. 'Jeff bought me a drink and I think I drank it down too quickly. I felt quite giddy after that dance.'

Whether she believed her or not, Venetia was eager to accept the explanation and smiled in delight. 'They dance well, don't they? Jeff is amazing. How do you like him?'

'He's OK—for a blind date,' Ginny added, her tone hardening. 'I thought we got past blind dates years ago. Why didn't you tell me Alex was bringing him along?'

'I wasn't sure if he was bringing a friend or who it would be—and anyway, I knew you'd only make a fuss. It was Alex's idea,' she added.

'Was it?' Ginny was openly disbelieving.

Venetia flushed. 'I just want you to be happy, too.'

'Do you? Well, in that case, you know what to do, don't you?'

'I'm not going to just hand Alex over to you, if that's what you mean,' Venetia retorted shortly.

'I saw him first,' Ginny pointed out, her voice rising.

But what looked as if it could have led to a very undignified mega-row was halted abruptly as the door was pushed open and a group of women came in. They exclaimed as soon as they saw the twins and came up to congratulate them and, inevitably, to remark on their likeness and ask the usual questions. 'Are you telepathic?' one asked.

'In some things,' Ginny answered, and without looking at Venetia, began to back towards the door, knowing that her twin was doing exactly the same.

Once outside they gave a gasp of relief. 'We ought to go and get our props loaded into the car,' Ginny remarked, not wanting to go back and dance.

Venetia looked at her and nodded. 'OK, I'll go and get Alex and Jeff to give us a hand.'

Their 'mirror' frame came to pieces and they were able to pack it and the rest of their props into the back of their old estate car. The men helped and Ginny expected that they would then go back to Colchester, but Venetia said, 'Why go home? Why not come back to the flat with us and have supper? You could even stay if you wanted to; we've got a sofa-bed you can sleep on. Then we can all spend the day together tomorrow.'

Ginny was stricken into silence by surprise; Venetia had never invited anyone to stay without asking her before. People had stayed, of course, loads of times, but they always made a point of asking—or telling— each other first.

Alex smiled at Venetia. 'That's a wonderful idea.'

But Jeff was looking at Ginny. 'It's kind of you, but maybe Ginny has other plans.'

They all looked at her and Ginny caught a wave of emotions; sympathy from Jeff, angry insistence from Venetia, and slight impatience from Alex. It was the impatience that decided her; she didn't want Alex to think badly of her even if it meant giving in to her twin's silent browbeating. Dragging up a smile, Ginny said, 'Of course, come to supper.' Deliberately she didn't say anything about staying the night, telling herself that Jeff might not want to anyway. She got into the driving seat of the car and leaned out of the window. 'You'll follow us, will you?'

But Venetia grabbed her opportunity. 'Jeff can go with you. I'd better go with Alex to show him the way.'

'Is that OK with you?' Jeff asked, coming to sit beside her.

'Yes, of course.' Ginny looked in the driving-mirror, waiting for Alex to come up behind them. 'I hope he follows me,' she said drily, 'because Venetia hasn't the faintest idea which way to go.'

Jeff laughed. 'Alex told me he'd once let Venetia drive his car, and swore he never would again. She nearly hit a tree.'

'Mm, she's a lousy driver,' Ginny agreed, her eyes still on the mirror.

'You're stronger than she is,' Jeff said, making it a definite statement.

Ginny turned her head to look at him with interest. 'How can you possibly tell that when you only met us tonight?'

He shrugged. 'It comes across. In little things. The way you supervised loading the car, your doing the driving.' He gave her a steady look. 'And the way you tried to hide your feelings about Alex.' She turned away, not saying anything, and Jeff said, his voice a little puzzled, 'I thought you'd only met Alex once before?'

No, Ginny thought, I met him first on the plane—and if I'd waited longer for him at Paris airport I would have got his message and he would never have mistaken Venetia for me. If only I'd waited. I'll never forgive myself for that, never.

'Ginny?'

'Mm?' She realised that Jeff was waiting for her to answer. 'Oh, sorry. Yes, I've only met him once before.' Headlights flashed behind her. 'Here they are,' she said with some relief. 'We can go now.'

It began to rain as they drove towards London, heavy driving rain that required all her concentration to drive safely. Occasionally she glanced in the rear-

view mirror to see if Alex was still following her; there
were headlights behind but whether it was Alex or not
was impossible to see. They stopped at a set of traffic
lights and the engine began to die. Ginny revved it up
and managed to prevent it stalling but as they went
on it began to miss and splutter.

'Er—I suppose you have got enough petrol?' Jeff
said diffidently.

Ginny gave him a look. 'That,' she said shortly, 'is
a typical male chauvinist question. Yes, there's plenty
of petrol; I filled it up on the way over tonight because I knew we would be late going home.'

'Sorry. Sounds like the carburettor, then.'

Even as he spoke the engine spluttered for a last
time and then fell silent. There was little traffic about
and Ginny was able to coast into the kerb. 'Hell!' she
said forcefully. 'Now I'll have to find a phone-box
and call the AA.'

'Don't worry. Alex will be able to fix it; he's a whizz
with anything mechanical.'

'If they're still behind us.'

'I'll see.' Turning up his coat collar, Jeff got out
of the car and went to stand at the kerb, waving Alex
down.

In a few moments Alex came and opened her door.
'Pull the bonnet clip, Ginny.' She did so, and the two
men peered into the engine, exchanged a few words,
and then Jeff got back in while Alex tinkered with
the engine.

'Alex wants you to take his car and drive Venetia
home. We'll follow when he's fixed the engine.'

Ginny shook her head. 'No, I'd better stay with the
car in case he can't fix it and we have to call out the
AA.'

'Fair enough. I'll drive Venetia home, then. You'd better give me directions.'

She did so, her heart thumping a little, and Jeff nodded, memorising them without having to note them down. He got out of the car again, spoke to Alex, then went back to the other car, but it was several minutes before it drove away. Minutes in which Venetia had put up a strong argument for staying, Ginny realised, but had been overridden by Jeff. Ginny smiled, thinking that she had found a friend in Jeff. Getting out of the car, she searched in the back to find a big, gaily striped umbrella, almost a sunshade, that they kept for emergencies like this, and went to hold it over Alex.

He glanced up. 'You'll get wet.'

'It doesn't matter.'

'Well, it certainly helps.' He bent over the engine again, lit by a convenient street-lamp, and went on drying out the leads with a piece of rag. The rain beat down on the umbrella and splashed on to the left side of her face, on to her feet and ankles. But Ginny didn't notice the rain; she felt absurdly happy, standing here with Alex, even if he was concentrating entirely on what he was doing. He straightened up and took the brolly from her. 'Try it now.'

It took a moment to start but when it did fire Ginny pushed down the throttle, revving up the engine to make sure it didn't stall again. Alex quickly slammed down the bonnet and got into the passenger-seat, throwing the umbrella in the back.

'Does it often break down?'

'Quite a bit,' Ginny admitted.

'You could do with a new car.'

'Can't afford one at the moment, I'm afraid. We've been saving up but something else always comes along that needs fixing or replacing. We had to buy a new fridge just before I went to Paris,' Ginny said without thinking.

'Paris?' Alex gave her a sharp look. 'I thought you went to Italy.'

'What?' Ginny suddenly realised the opportunity was there, waiting for her to take. For a moment she caught her breath, imagining what this could lead to. But a vision of Venetia came into her mind and she knew her twin would never believe that it had happened purely by accident. Slowly she said, 'Oh, yes. But I went to Paris, too. Last—last autumn.'

'You girls certainly get around.' He glanced at her averted profile. 'You can stop revving the engine and drive on now.'

'Right.' Ginny found first gear and moved out into the road, very aware that this was the first time that she had really been alone with Alex. She would have liked to try and impress him with her wit and conversational abilities, and ordinarily she was far from tongue-tied, but now she couldn't find anything to say. She just wanted to go on, driving along like this forever.

His voice amused, Alex said, 'Aren't you going to change gear?'

'Yes, I suppose so.' She did so and gave him a direct look. 'You make me nervous.'

'I do?' He was genuinely surprised. 'I thought you two girls were far too sophisticated to be nervous of anyone.'

'I'm not talking about Venetia, I'm talking about me.'

Alex was silent for a moment, then said, 'Venetia hinted to me that you might be jealous.'

'She—she did?' Ginny could hardly believe it, amazed that Venetia would ever have taken the risk of letting him know that she was interested. Already regretting her earlier decision not to tell him the truth, Ginny said, 'Yes, as a matter of fact, I—I think I am.'

'It's entirely natural, I suppose,' Alex astounded her by saying.

'Is it?' She gave him a dazed glance, never having thought him to be narcissistic.

'When you're as close to someone as you are to Venetia, it's bound to come as rather a blow when she begins to care for someone else.'

So they had been talking at cross purposes. Annoyed with herself for not realising, Ginny said shortly, 'Has Venetia said that she cares for you, then?'

He hesitated for a moment, then said steadily, 'Yes, she has.' Adding deliberately, 'And I care for her—very much.'

'Do you, now?' Ginny could hear the waspishness in her own voice but she couldn't help it. She was angry with him for spoiling their first time alone together, angry with herself for not telling him the truth when she had the chance. 'You fell in love with her when you met her on the plane, I suppose.'

'I was very attracted to her,' Alex admitted, with no conception of how that implied denial had devastated Ginny. He went on, 'I was terribly disappointed when I thought I'd lost her and was determined to find her again. But it's since we've been going out together these last few weeks that I've really started to care for her.'

'I see,' Ginny said tightly. 'And you're warning me to keep out of your way, are you?'

'You can't hold on to Venetia forever, Ginny,' he said gently. 'You have to let go—for your own sake as well as hers.'

She gave a harsh laugh. 'You think so, do you? You should have been a doctor of philosophy as well as physics.'

His voice becoming angry, Alex said, 'I'm not going to let you come between us, Ginny. You're going to have to learn to be one person—not part of a pair. I intend to become a very important part of Venetia's life.'

She stopped at a traffic light, braking hard at the last minute and almost stalling the engine again. Jerking on the handbrake, she turned to face him. 'You're a blind fool, Alex. You've only known Venetia a few weeks. You can't possibly be sure of your feelings in that time.' It sounded convincing when she said it, but at the same moment she realised that she was sure of her own feelings, so why shouldn't he be sure of his? In an agony of emotion she said, 'You can't even tell us apart. If Venetia wasn't around you'd feel the same way about me.'

Alex thought she was just trying to persuade him that his feelings were false. 'You're mistaken,' he said shortly. 'I was attracted to her first by her looks, of course. But it's her entire personality, her whole being that I care for now. You might fool me for a few moments, but not for long.'

Desperate now, Ginny said forcefully, 'No, it's you who's mistaken. Venetia isn't—Venetia isn't the girl you think.'

Alex's face grew very cold and there was disgust in his voice as he said, 'And nor are you, it seems. How can you possibly stoop so low as to malign your own sister?'

'You don't understand. I didn't mean——'

He looked away. 'The lights are green.'

She stared at his averted profile for a moment, then, slowly putting the car into gear, Ginny drove on. They were almost at the flat. Everything had gone so terribly wrong. She had been given a precious half-hour with Alex, even an opportunity to tell him the truth, but somehow it had all hopelessly backfired. They had got their lines crossed and ended up having a row that must have completely alienated him. Their building came into sight and she pulled up in the forecourt. 'Alex?' She turned to look at him, wondering whether there was still time to tell him the truth.

'Well?' The face he turned to her was cold and implacable.

She took one look at it and her heart sank like a cold grey stone in a greyer sea. 'Nothing,' she mumbled, and turned away, unwilling to let him see her despair.

CHAPTER FOUR

ALEX and Ginny got silently out of the estate car, avoiding looking at each other. Alex's car was already in the car park and the light was showing in the sitting-room of the flat. Usually they immediately unloaded their props, afraid of having them stolen, but tonight Ginny didn't even give them a thought. She led the way to the main door, unlocked it and went upstairs to the flat.

Venetia ran to the door as soon as she heard Ginny's key in the lock. Her eyes were anxious and afraid, going first to Alex and then to Ginny. A terrified look came into them as she saw Alex's set face, followed by amazement and relief when she saw the chagrin in Ginny's and realised that they'd had a row. Breaking into a smile, Venetia said with sisterly concern, 'You poor darling, you're soaked. Go and get dry. And Alex, let me take your jacket.'

She fussed around them, pushing Alex into the bathroom to wash his hands and Ginny into her bedroom to change. Ginny was glad to go; she would have liked to stay there all night. She towelled her hair dry and took off the red velvet dress; it would need to be cleaned, she decided, before it could be worn again. Putting on tight-fitting jeans and a blue sweater, she brushed her hair until it hung long, loose and glistening down her back, curling at the ends from the damp. She didn't want to join the others, but it had to be faced. When she came out of her room she

79

went first to the kitchen. Venetia was there and had also changed into jeans and a blue sweater. She was very happy as she cooked supper for them, Alex leaning against the wall and neither of them minding that his large figure took up almost all the space in the fitted kitchen. He glanced up as Ginny came in, met her eyes sardonically, then looked away to drink from the glass of beer he was holding.

'Want any help?' Ginny offered.

'You can set the table, if you like.' Venetia was bubblingly happy, not knowing how it had happened, and wisely not asking, but sure that Alex and Ginny had had a mega-row, which could do her nothing but good.

Ginny collected knives and forks and mats and went into the living-room. Jeff was sitting in an armchair, reading the paper, his long legs stretched out in front of him so that she had to step over them to reach the table. He glanced up at her. 'Sorry, Venetia.'

'I'm Ginny.'

'Oh.' His eyes searched her face. 'You OK?'

'Of course. Fine.'

Her tone made him put aside the paper and get to his feet. 'Can I help at all?'

'No, thanks.' She went over to the sideboard to get some glasses but he was in the way. 'Excuse me.'

'Ginny?'

'What?'

'Want to talk about it?'

Her shortness should have warned him. Swinging round on him, her voice rose angrily as Ginny said, 'No. I don't want to talk about it with you. Why the hell should I?' But then she broke off as she saw Alex come into the room.

He paused in the doorway, his eyes searching their faces, a frown of anger coming into them at her scathing tone. 'Is this the way you usually treat your guests?' he asked, his voice icy. 'But then, that's about what I should expect from you.'

Biting her lip, Ginny turned away, fighting back tears. Then she was amazed to hear Jeff say roughly, 'Leave her alone, Alex.'

Slowly turning, Ginny found the two men facing each other. Jeff's chin was thrust forward and Alex was staring at him in surprise. But then Alex shrugged in tacit acceptance. Walking over to the table, he put the bottle of wine he was carrying on to it. 'Venetia said the corkscrew is in here.'

It was the strangest meal, each of them trying to hide strong but different emotions, with the result that all conversation was short and unnatural. Ginny was very aware of Alex's disapproval whenever he happened to glance at her, and he wasn't too pleased with Jeff either, instead devoting his attention to Venetia, who glowed under it. Jeff did his best to keep the conversation general but didn't have much luck with Ginny, who mostly gazed down at the food she was pushing round her plate instead of eating. Venetia was the only one who was enjoying herself, and so obviously that Ginny could have hit her.

The meal over, they cleared the table and pulled out the sofa-bed. 'Jeff can sleep on this,' Venetia announced. 'And Alex can have my bed. I'll go in with Ginny.'

'Maybe it would be better if we went home,' Jeff suggested.

But Venetia wanted them—or at least she wanted Alex—to stay, and she had her way without too much argument. Ginny didn't say anything, just went into the kitchen to wash the dishes while they sorted themselves out. Jeff followed her in a few minutes later and picked up the drying cloth.

'You don't have to do that,' Ginny said shortly. 'You're a guest.'

'I want to.'

They worked silently for a few moments until Ginny sighed and said, 'I'm sorry I snapped at you earlier.'

'It was my fault, I should have minded my own business. Look, if you'd rather I went home it's not too late to say.'

'No, of course you must stay.' Ginny hesitated, then said frankly, 'It isn't so bad when you're here—I don't feel such a gooseberry.' Seeing his mouth twist a little, she quickly added, 'And we haven't really had a chance to talk to each other, have we?'

Jeff gave a small laugh. 'No, we seem to have missed out that stage.'

Ordinarily when people stayed overnight they would sit up talking into the small hours, but tonight Ginny said almost immediately that she was tired and the party broke up. The girls used the bathroom first and Venetia brought her night things from her room to Ginny's. There was tenseness between them as they undressed and neither spoke until they had got into bed and the light was out. The bed was only four feet wide but they contrived to lie near the edges so that they weren't touching, until Venetia sighed, 'This is silly,' and reached out to grasp Ginny's hand.

For a moment Ginny resisted, but then returned the pressure.

'What do you want to do tomorrow?' Venetia asked. 'We could go for a walk on Hampstead Heath

if it isn't raining. And there's a concert at the Albert
Hall in the afternoon.'

'Yes, sure, whatever you like,' Ginny said without
interest.

'I think Jeff's nice, don't you? He has hidden
depths.'

'He's OK.' They were silent for a few moments, but
Venetia's unspoken question came across so strongly
that Ginny said irritably, 'No, I didn't tell Alex the
truth.'

Venetia sighed. 'I didn't think you could have,
although all the way back home I was afraid you
would. Why didn't you?'

'I almost did,' Ginny admitted. 'He gave me the
opportunity.'

'But you didn't take it,' Venetia said with
satisfaction.

Ginny lay silently, not wanting to talk, her thoughts
going back over the car ride with Alex, trying to find
where it had all gone wrong. But she could almost
feel Venetia digging into her mind, looking for
reasons, and, as always when they were alone together
without any outside distractions, their minds were
close.

'You and Alex quarrelled over me,' Venetia said
with certainty. 'But why if you didn't tell him?' Ginny
was silent, not wanting her to guess, but after a few
moments Venetia went on, her tone a half-murmur,
'Alex was angry with you, not me, and the only reason
he could have for being angry with you is if—yes, is
if he's guessed that you don't want us to go out together. Perhaps he thinks that you're angry because
he's threatening to come between us.' She gave a little
crow of triumphant laughter. 'Of course, that must

be it.' She gave a happy, comfortable sigh. 'So now
I don't have to worry about you any more.'

'I can still tell him the truth.'

'But you won't,' Venetia said firmly. 'You had your
chance and you didn't take it. And even if you told
him now he'd never believe you; he'd think that you
were just trying to split us up.'

'But I could prove to him that I was telling the
truth,' Ginny said shortly.

'How?'

'By reminding him of things we talked about on
the plane, things you don't know about.'

'He'll have forgotten by now,' Venetia said
scoffingly.

'No.' It was Ginny's turn to be certain. 'He won't
ever forget.'

This disconcerted Venetia and they lay silently again
for a while, and it was inevitable that their thoughts
should go to Alex. Was he lying awake in the room
on the other side of the wall? Ginny wondered. Was
he lying in Venetia's bed, thinking about her, wishing
he was with her? Was there an ache of frustrated
longing deep down inside him, the same kind of ache
that Ginny was feeling now—and Venetia, too?

'I haven't been to bed with him yet,' Venetia said,
reading her thoughts.

'I know.'

'You can't know.'

'Yes, I can. And I'll know when you do sleep with
him.'

Venetia turned on to her side, her back to Ginny.
'I wish we weren't so close,' she said exasperatedly,
but she meant mentally, not physically.

It occurred to Ginny that Venetia would probably use Alex's annoyance with her to drive an even bigger wedge between them. She would encourage and feed the idea that Ginny was afraid of Alex's splitting them up until Ginny would be able to do nothing about it. It seemed as if she had won before Ginny had even started to put up a fight.

Ginny, too, turned on her side, pulling the duvet up close around her. This is just a skirmish, she told herself. I'll fight—and I'll win. And by fair means or foul? All's fair in love and war; that kind of thing? Why not? she thought in a fleeting instant of bleak resentment—Venetia certainly had. But the thought troubled her; how could love and romance be a delight to remember if it was based on cheating? How could you have a trusting relationship when there would always be a secret to hide? Had Venetia thought of that—or was she so crazy about Alex that she didn't care how she got him? She must be, presumably. Knowing her twin, Ginny guessed that Venetia was so starry-eyed that she hadn't given a thought to the distant future; she probably hadn't looked past an engagement ring and wedding-bells. The thought of a wedding between Venetia and Alex made her grit her teeth. Damn it, she thought fiercely, I will *not* trail down the aisle as Venetia's bridesmaid and watch her marry the man I love. I'll do everything I can to get him for myself first.

This thought stayed in Ginny's mind until she fell asleep and was the first thing that came to her when she woke up the next morning. It was early, Venetia was still asleep and the flat was quiet. Slipping carefully out of bed, Ginny took a tracksuit from her drawer and went into the bathroom to change into it.

To reach the front door she had to go through the living-room. Jeff was still fast asleep, but he was too big for the sofa-bed; his bare feet hung over the end. His long fair eyelashes brushed his cheeks, giving him a youthful, vulnerable look. As she edged her way past him the door to Venetia's bedroom opened and Alex came out. He went to speak but she put a finger up to her lips, gesturing down at Jeff.

Alex grinned and mouthed, 'Going jogging?' Ginny nodded and went to tell him who she was but he held up his spread fingers. 'Five minutes.' And went back into the bedroom.

She hesitated, wondering whether to go without him; he certainly wouldn't want to go with her when he realised who she was. But she turned and went into the kitchen, ran herself a glass of water while she waited. She'd noticed last night that both Jeff and Alex had overnight bags with them, so they must have been prepared to stay even though Venetia had tried to make her invitation sound spontaneous. When Alex came to find her a few minutes later he was wearing a navy tracksuit and running shoes, sweat-bands round his wrists.

'OK?' he asked, poking his head round the door as she was drinking. 'Let's go,' and turned away before she could answer.

They crept through the living-room and out of the front door, Alex running ahead of her down the stairs and out of the main door.

'Which way?' he asked on the pavement.

'The park's over that way. You have to go down the street and through an alleyway to reach it,' Ginny told him, pointing. 'But Alex——' She caught his arm as he went to run across the road, and looked steadily into his face. 'I'm Ginny, not Venetia.'

His head swung round as he stared at her. 'Venetia has a tracksuit exactly like that,' he said accusingly.

'I know. They were given to us after a sports promotion we took part in.'

She waited, expecting him to turn and go back inside, but after a frowning moment he said, 'We'd better get started, then.'

There were other Sunday-morning joggers in the park, some of whom Ginny knew by sight and who waved or called out a greeting. Alex set a fast pace but Ginny was young and fit and had no difficulty in keeping up with him. He didn't speak until someone going in the other direction called, 'Hi, Ginny,' as she passed.

'How do they know it's you?' he demanded.

'Venetia never jogs this early in the morning.'

'Why not?'

'She doesn't get up in time.'

They came to a weed-encrusted pond and Ginny went over to its edge to feed the family of ducks who lived there with some bread she had in her pocket. Alex came over and stood beside her, watched as she bent to very gently stroke one of the ducklings with her fingertip.

'I'm surprised they let you do that,' he commented.

'Oh, I was bitten a few times at first but they're used to me now. This is their second family; the first was killed by some boys,' Ginny said with anger in her voice.

He glanced at her face as she stood up and threw the last of the bread far out in the pond so that the ducks went quacking after it. She went to run on but he said, 'I think we have to talk.'

'Do we?' She found herself suddenly nervous, wondering if this was to be more recriminations or some form of reconciliation.

Apparently it was the latter because Alex said, 'I'm sorry if I was abrupt with you yesterday. You were honest enough to tell me you were jealous of my relationship with Venetia and I ought to have respected you for that.' He turned away to look at the ducks. 'But, you see, it's rather difficult for a man when he comes up against sisters as close as you. You must realise that yourself.'

'Yes, we are close,' Ginny admitted. She was watching him, wondering if she could in some way let him know how she felt, that he'd made a mistake in thinking her jealous of him.

He shot her a glance. 'And I suppose you think, quite rightly, that we haven't known each other very long. But, for my part, I'm very attracted to Venetia; in fact I've never felt like this about any other girl before.'

'Have you told her that?' Ginny asked uneasily.

Alex frowned, but then nodded curtly, 'Of course.' Ginny's heart sank a little and she looked away, feeling in her pocket for any last breadcrumbs, but her head swung round as Alex went on, 'I think it was almost love at first sight.'

'You mean—from the moment you met on the plane?' Hardly daring to breathe, she gazed intently into his face.

His mouth curved in a reminiscent smile. 'Yes, I rather think so. The attraction was so great that I realise now that it must have been love, even then.' He lifted his eyes to hers. 'I don't want to be your enemy, Ginny. I want Venetia, yes, but you'll always be her sister. Perhaps you'll always be closer to her than I am. Until you meet someone yourself, at least.'

Trying desperately to still the fast beating of her heart at his admission, Ginny took a deep breath, then frowned, wondering why he was telling her all this. But as realisation dawned her brow cleared. 'You're afraid of losing Venetia if you alienate me?'

He made a wry face. 'I certainly don't want to have to force her into choosing between us, yes.'

If you only knew, Ginny thought with heavy irony; Venetia made her choice the first time she met you. But she wasn't about to tell Alex that.

'You're mistaken about me,' she said, feeling her way, terrified of saying the wrong thing, but so wanting him to know the truth, especially as he had admitted falling in love with her at first sight.

Alex's eyebrows rose quizzically. 'I hope so,' he said frankly. 'I'd hate to think that you would deliberately try to break us up and prevent Venetia's happiness. I know that the fact that you work together and make every use of being identical twins is a great financial advantage to you, but——'

'I'm not worried about the money side of it,' Ginny broke in hotly.

'No?' He sounded sceptical.

'No. I can make a career for myself, if I have to. Believe it or not, being twins isn't always an asset where work is concerned. In fact, I've been thinking lately that maybe it might be better if we split up.'

His brows rose in surprise and pleasure. 'So why, then?' Alex gave her a direct look out of his grey eyes, waiting for her to answer.

But answering wasn't easy. After a moment Ginny said, 'I have a right to my own happiness.'

'Of course, but not when it means preventing someone else from being happy. As you say, it's about time you and Venetia split, in your own lives as well as where work is concerned.'

'Possibly,' she agreed tentatively. 'But for the right reasons.'

His voice hardened. 'And is Venetia's falling in love with me a wrong reason?'

'No. But are sure that you're in love with *her*?' Ginny put as much emphasis as she could on the word, hoping that he would see what she was getting at without her spelling it out.

But Alex only frowned. 'I've already said that I am. Look, I'm not going to rush Venetia into anything, if that's what you're afraid of. I know that we haven't known each other long and I'll give her time to be sure of her own mind.'

'And for you to be sure of her,' Ginny pointed out. 'You—you really don't know her very well.'

A steely look came into his eyes. 'I hope you're not going to make any insinuations as you did last night, or you and I are going back to being enemies.'

Seeing that she was beating her head against a brick wall, Ginny sighed. 'No.' She lifted her eyes to meet his and spoke earnestly, 'But please remember that Venetia and I are identical to look at. We could—we do sometimes take each other's place. And...' She paused, wondering whether to go that far or not, but licking lips gone dry, eventually said, 'And our feelings are nearly always the same, too.'

'Possibly they are, but...' Alex's voice faltered as the idea hit him. He gave her a sharp look, meeting her eager eyes, but then immediately looked away and gave a strongly definite, negative shake of the head, completely rejecting the idea that she might care about him. He glanced at his watch. 'We'd better get going.'

They began to jog again, Alex running silently at her side. But after a while, Ginny said, 'Whose idea was it to bring Jeff along yesterday?'

Before answering, Alex ducked under the branch of a tree that Ginny hadn't even noticed was low before. He shrugged as much as one could while running. 'Venetia and I just thought it would be nice to make up a four, that was all.'

'But who suggested it?'

'Does it matter?'

'As I was the one Jeff was brought along for, then, yes, I think it does.'

'Don't you like him?'

'That isn't the point. If it was Venetia's idea then she had no right to do it without asking me first.'

'And if it was my idea?'

They came out of the park and had to wait at a pedestrian crossing for the lights to change. Ginny turned to look at him. His hair was damp and there was a faint stubble on his chin where he hadn't had time to shave. To her he looked wonderful. Her heart did a great lurch and for a moment she couldn't speak.

'Well?' he said impatiently.

Making a great effort, she answered, 'You shouldn't have pushed a stranger on to me to try and make up for your being with Venetia. That wasn't—kind.'

'Aren't you making a big thing of it?'

'I don't think so. Venetia knows we never go out on blind dates, and she should have told you so.'

His voice becoming harsh, Alex said, 'She was only thinking of you, but, all right, I promise to remember in future. But Jeff came along to escort you willingly enough, so do me a favour, will you, and don't take it out on him?' The lights changed to red and the cars stopped to let them cross.

When they reached the other side, Ginny said, 'Jeff is OK. I just don't like having men provided for me, that's all. I'm capable of attracting men for myself.' She shot him a look and said forcefully, '*You* should know that.'

'Because I was attracted to Venetia, do you mean?' he asked, not understanding.

'No, that isn't what I meant at all.' They reached the flat and Ginny took the key from her pocket. Giving him a direct look, she said, 'Think about it. Remember what I said,' and turned away to open the door.

The others were having breakfast, a delicious smell of fried bacon filling the flat. Venetia jumped up and went to kiss Alex. 'All this energy,' she exclaimed. 'You should have woken us and we would have come with you.'

'You might have, but I wouldn't,' Jeff put in. 'I need to put on weight, not lose it, which is why I'm going to have another helping of bacon and eggs.'

Ginny went off to shower and change, as did Alex. She was sitting down and having breakfast when he joined them, coming to sit opposite her. She shot him a swift look, but he seemed deliberately to avoid her eyes, instead putting his arm round Venetia's waist as she brought a plate of bacon and eggs and mushrooms for him.

'I know you like mushrooms,' she said.

'You spoil me.' He pulled her down to kiss her and afterwards smiled into her eyes. 'Good morning, my darling.'

'Good morning.' Her voice was husky and her eyes rapturous as she put her arms round Alex's neck and slipped on to his lap.

Jeff looked at Ginny. 'I'm glad I've finished my breakfast or those two would put me off my food.'

Alex laughed and looked round. 'Nothing puts you off your food. What shall we do today?'

Venetia immediately put in her idea for a walk on Hampstead Heath, but Jeff said there was a new exhibition on at the Victoria and Albert Museum that he wanted to see, while Alex wanted to visit Catherine Dock to see a fleet of sailing ships that were gathered there. Ginny didn't join in the discussion; she knew that Alex had deliberately shown his feelings for Venetia so openly for her benefit. So that she wouldn't get any ideas, presumably.

But she had made him think. They went to Catherine Dock; Venetia, wanting to please Alex, said that the ships wouldn't be there for long and they could always go to the Heath another time, and they went on to the museum in the afternoon. Several times during the day Ginny surprised Alex's eyes on her, a puzzled expression in their depths. She let a challenge show in her glance, and he didn't look away when his eyes clashed with hers; he wasn't the type to pretend or hide his feelings. But he wasn't close to guessing the truth—Ginny could see that too, unfortunately. Perhaps he didn't want to believe it. Perhaps it was too impossible for him to imagine.

Venetia knew that something had happened between them and her chin thrust forward determinedly. She gave Ginny angry looks behind Alex's back and redoubled her efforts to keep him by her side. Not that she had to try very hard; Alex was quite happy to be always with her. Which left Jeff and Ginny to keep each other amused. Luckily Jeff was an interesting companion so it wasn't hard to do, especially at the museum where he talked knowledgeably to Ginny about the exhibition. So eruditely, in fact, that a group of tourists thought he was a guide and walked round with them. They both saw the funny side of this and Jeff played on the poor tourists shamefully, making Ginny crease up with scarcely suppressed laughter, which she was at last able to release as they left the exhibition.

Alex and Venetia were waiting outside and looked at them in astonishment as they both howled with laughter.

'What's so funny?' Venetia demanded, not wanting to miss anything.

'Jeff's impression of a learned guide. Those poor people. Even I know that clock faces with Roman numerals weren't made exclusively by the descendants of the Roman legions who settled in England. Fancy telling them they had the franchise. You did it so po-facedly, too. Shame on you,' she admonished, but laughing as she looked up at Jeff.

The others laughed too, but Ginny caught them giving her a speculative look. Did she only have to share a laugh with Jeff for them to hope that she was falling for him? Ginny thought with annoyance.

They all had dinner together in a restaurant near the museum and then it was time to go back to the flat for the men to collect their gear and drive back to Colchester. Ginny went down to the main door to see them off but Alex and Venetia stayed behind so that they could say goodbye in private.

'I'm afraid this hasn't been a pleasant weekend for you,' Jeff remarked as he dumped his bag in the back of the car. 'I'm sorry.'

'No, please. It's my fault. I . . .' But Ginny found it impossible to explain and shrugged, her eyes shadowing. 'It's just one of those things, that's all.'

'I meant that I'm sorry you didn't find it pleasant because I would very much like to see you again,' Jeff corrected her.

Ginny flushed. 'That's very sweet of you. But surely. . .' She gave him a troubled look.

Jeff gave a short laugh. 'I like you, Ginny. And I think you've got guts. If I can help you in any way, even by your using me, then go ahead and do it.'

She shook her head. 'You deserve better than that.'

He pushed his glasses up his nose. 'Maybe I could use a friend, too.'

'You could? Really?'

He nodded. 'A no-strings, hands-off, safe-distance, no-emotions type of friendship.' He grinned. 'How does that sound to you?'

Too good to be true, Ginny thought. She gave him a contemplative look, wondering if this was a line, one that she'd heard before. But Jeff seemed too nice for that, so maybe he was getting over an affair and friendship was really all he wanted. She nodded and smiled. 'OK, we'll give it a go.' And she held out her hand to him.

Jeff shook it just as the other two came out of the building. There was a bemused look on Venetia's face, as if she had been well and truly kissed, but Alex noticed the handshake and gave them an appraising glance, his eyebrows flickering when he saw Jeff's grin. Throwing his bag in the back, Alex gave Venetia a last kiss and lifted a hand in farewell. 'Bye, Ginny. Be seeing you, I expect.' For a moment their eyes met, but Alex's were cool and casual. What she had tried to tell him hadn't made the slightest difference.

She moved to stand beside her twin, and they watched the car as it pulled away, Venetia waving until it turned the corner. 'So that's over,' Ginny said heavily.

Venetia sighed. 'Yes, I'm afraid it is. I won't see him again until next weekend.' Reluctantly she turned to go in, but stopped on the step and faced Ginny, her chin coming up. 'And I don't want you around next time I see him—so just keep out of the way.'

She swung round and strode inside but Ginny followed more slowly. She's frightened, she thought. She knows I can still break them up. But why should she feel that way when Alex had so openly shown what he felt for her? But perhaps it was *because* he had done so so openly; if he hadn't felt that he needed to prove it to Ginny he might have kept his feelings to himself for a while longer. So had all she achieved been to push them more closely together? Ginny wondered bitterly. But whether it had or not it had definitely come between herself and Venetia.

The rift between them didn't heal at once, but they were busy work-wise that week and had to co-operate with one another. On the Tuesday they were booked to appear at the opening of a new knitting yarn shop in Tonbridge called 'Twin-set', and on Thursday they travelled up to the television studios in Birmingham to take part in a quiz show, competing against a set of male twins. It was an afternoon show so the prize money wasn't very high, but it gave them some publicity and they won two hundred and fifty pounds, plus having all their expenses paid, so it was an extremely useful day. The only drawback was that they had to go up by train because the car wouldn't start.

'We'll have to get a new one,' Ginny said worriedly on the journey back. 'We can't take the risk of its letting us down on the way to a job.'

'I thought that was the idea of joining the AA. They come out and fix it for you if it breaks down.'

'They do, but you usually have to wait ages, and you still have to buy spare parts and tyres and batteries. I think the best thing we can do is sell the Ford and use the money and our savings as a deposit on as new a car as we can afford. The trouble is we need an estate car for our props.' Ginny looked at Venetia. 'Unless we got a van, of course; you can get those cheaply and it would solve all our problems.'

'We can't turn up to do a cabaret act in a van,' Venetia said firmly. 'It would look all wrong.'

'Well, we're going to have to buy a new battery for it tomorrow anyway; we have those two cabaret bookings on Friday and Saturday nights.'

'Can't we tell the agency not to get us bookings for Saturdays? I like to go out with Alex at the weekend,' Venetia complained.

Ginny shot her a look. 'It's our main source of income, you know that.'

Venetia pouted. 'Maybe I'll call up Alex and ask his advice about the car. He'll know what to do.'

'We already know what to do,' Ginny pointed out shortly. 'We just haven't got the money to do it.'

But when Alex called that evening, as he did nearly every evening, Ginny could hear Venetia telling him all about the car, and when she put the phone down she said with satisfaction, 'Alex agrees we need a new car, but he said that second-hand cars are much cheaper round Colchester than they are in London, so he's going to look out for a good one for us.'

'Did you tell him we haven't got much money to spend?'

'Of course, don't worry. Alex knows what he's doing.'

And it seemed that he did, because that Sunday he arrived driving a late model metallic silver estate car that was in extremely good condition. Jeff followed, driving Alex's car.

'It's gorgeous. Just what we need. You are clever, darling.' And Venetia put her arms round his neck to give Alex an exuberant hug.

Getting into the driving seat, Ginny looked at the milometer. 'It's only done nine thousand miles,' she exclaimed. 'And it's almost new.' Jumping out of the car, she went over to Alex. 'How much did it cost?'

She looked up at him with a worried frown; she had always been the treasurer of the twins and knew that they couldn't possibly afford anything as good as this.

'Four thousand,' he told her. 'I paid for it so that you could have it straight away, but you can give me what you get for your car and pay the rest back when you can.'

He went to turn away but Ginny caught his arm. 'I'm not a fool, Alex; the current retail price for a car like this is nearer ten thousand.'

'The price is four thousand; I bought it from an American professor at the university who's been called home and wanted to get rid of it in a hurry.'

She gazed up into his face, searching it. 'I don't believe you,' she said flatly. 'And we don't need charity.'

Her voice had risen a little and a grim look came into Alex's eyes. Taking hold of her arm, he pulled her away from the others. 'All right, so you're no fool, but just remember that last weekend your car broke down late at night, and if I hadn't been there to fix it one of you would have had to walk to a phone to get help. Anything might have happened to you. And I don't want to run any risk of that happening to Venetia—or you. So now do you understand?'

Ginny's body stiffened. 'Quite. What about interest on your loan?'

'There is no interest.' His grey eyes looked directly into hers. 'Venetia is my girl; of course I wouldn't charge any interest. And I don't want her to know about this, because she'd feel obliged to be grateful—do you understand? I'm happy to do it for her.'

He didn't add 'and you' this time, she noticed. Ginny nodded woodenly. 'All right.' She didn't thank him because she didn't feel grateful. He had done it for Venetia but he had bound Ginny not to tell her, which had made yet another secret between them.

The four of them spent the afternoon together at a concert at the Albert Hall, driving there in the new car so that Ginny would have a chance to get used to it. Alex sat beside her, which was a mixed blessing, but Ginny was such a natural driver that he seldom had to guide her. And at least he told her so when they arrived, which brought a swift rush of colour to her cheeks. Alex went to get the tickets but could only get two sets of two seats, so Venetia and Alex naturally went off together. Ginny couldn't help wondering if Alex had fixed it that way, but she didn't mind sitting with Jeff and they made no attempt to find the others in the interval.

Alex managed to get up to London a couple of times in the next week, and he also took Venetia out at the weekend, as they didn't have a cabaret engagement. Venetia didn't tell Ginny her plans and she met Alex in town so that Ginny didn't see him. Deliberately keeping them apart, Ginny realised.

It was time to give some thought to her own future, but she was reluctant to do so, because she didn't want to envisage a future for herself in which Alex had no part—or at least a more important part than that of a brother-in-law. But whenever Venetia came home after seeing him she was shining with happiness and it seemed as if nothing could ever come between them.

Ginny had dates, too, during those two weeks, and Jeff came up to London a couple of times to see her, but although Ginny tried to enjoy herself—perhaps tried too hard—she couldn't help comparing the men to Alex and wondering what it would be like if she were with him instead. Seeing the way Venetia looked after a date with him became a real, physical pain, so bad that she began to go to bed before Venetia came home, a thing that she had never done before. But then, they were both doing a lot of things that they had never done before.

The modelling assignment that Simon Blake had fixed for her came round; two days of work at a stately home, shooting winter tweeds for the forthcoming autumn issue of a country-living type magazine.

'Have they found you a nice hotel to stay in?' Venetia asked casually, the day before.

Ginny gave her a surprised look. 'We don't need a hotel. I'll be able to come home every night; the shoot is just outside London.'

'Oh, is it?' Venetia carefully controlled her voice so that it was difficult to judge her emotions. 'I thought you'd have to stay.'

So that she could invite Alex to stay at the flat? Ginny immediately wondered. So that they could go to bed together for the first time? Venetia must want him very badly if she was willing to bring him here; it was hardly a very romantic setting, and not one that Ginny would have chosen for such a wonderful night. Perhaps Venetia was eager to deepen her relationship with Alex by making him her lover. But strangely she hadn't sounded too put out.

'Sorry to disappoint you,' Ginny said shortly, 'but I shall be coming home.'

Luckily the weather was fine for the shoot, the spring sunshine filtering through the bare branches of the long avenue of mature oak trees that led to the Georgian mansion. It was good to be modelling again, Ginny had almost forgotten how good. She fitted back into the crew and moved in front of Simon's camera with all the naturalness in the world. She didn't have a chance to be alone with him until they finished working on the first evening.

'Made up your mind?' he asked her.

Ginny hadn't until that moment, but she gave an impulsive nod. 'Yes. I'd like to take you up on your offer, please.'

'Good. I'm going abroad again next week but give me your home number and I'll let you know when we can start. Be thinking about the type of shots you want.'

'Right.'

She felt better after making the decision. And it had been so simple; Simon hadn't mentioned it again and nor had she. And Ginny didn't tell Venetia when she got home. The decision seemed to be lucky for her, too, because Simon recommended her to some editors and she got several assignments for herself alone as well as the usual kind of things with Venetia. It was natural that Venetia should be a little jealous; they had always tossed for individual assignments before, but these editors had been told the situation and specified Ginny.

'It looks as if that assignment in Paris really worked for you,' Venetia said with a pout.

'Well, it didn't do you any harm in a roundabout way,' Ginny pointed out. 'Take one of the jobs if you want it so badly.'

But Venetia shook her head. 'That would be cheating.'

Ginny gave her a sardonic look. 'So what's new?'

Venetia glared at her and walked out of the room, but the conversation had given Ginny an idea that wouldn't go away however hard she tried to suppress it—and she really ought to have suppressed it because it wouldn't be playing fair. But then Venetia hadn't played fair either.

They had a book in which they noted all their engagements. Ginny duly entered all that she had been asked to do, but made one false entry, not of date but of place. She had a terrible guilt feeling as she did it, but comforted herself with the thought that she could always tell Venetia that the venue had been changed. It was a week away, but in that week Venetia deliberately turned down a job that Ginny had got for them both because she was going out with Alex. Also Venetia made a big thing of not taking any work for herself because it would mean leaving Ginny alone in the flat while she was away, a thing that she jealously avoided. Angered, Ginny decided to go ahead with her ploy and got the agency to phone her while she was at home about a trivial query.

Venetia answered the phone, thinking it might be Alex, but handed the receiver to Ginny. 'It's the agency. More work, I suppose.'

Ginny took the call, but after a few moments put her hand over the mouthpiece. 'They've got a last-minute job for me, but it's on the same couple of days that I'm working for Simon Blake. It sounds really good. Modelling clothes for the Panache catalogue. Do you want to take it instead?'

Venetia stood up. 'You're going to be away at the same time?'

Ginny nodded, hoping that Venetia wouldn't guess she was play-acting.

'OK, I'll take it,' Venetia said excitedly.

Ginny had banked on her being unable to resist a shoot like that; she regretted having to give it up herself, but hopefully it would be worth it. The day they were due to leave for their assignments—one real, one not—Ginny drove Venetia to the station and saw her off, staying till the train was safely out of sight. Her heart was beating fast and she felt terribly guilty; never in her life had she even thought of deceiving her twin before. A dozen times on the journey to the station she had almost blurted out the truth, but the sense of being so unfairly used herself held her back.

But as Ginny walked back through the station the guilt seemed to float from her and join the sparrows that flew under the huge dome. Her footsteps quickened until she was almost running, and the traffic warden who had started to write her out a parking ticket got such a dazzling smile that he let her drive away without it.

Waiting until lunchtime was an agony, but as soon as Ginny knew that Alex would be free she called him at the university. He was brought to the phone almost at once. 'Hi,' she said, trying desperately not to let her nervous excitement show. 'Guess who this is?'

'I thought you were on a shoot.'

'It was cancelled at the last minute. The photographer was taken ill.'

'So you'll be home—and Ginny is away?' Alex's voice was full of anticipation.

Avoiding telling a deliberate lie, she said, 'Can you get away tonight?'

'Nothing would stop me. See you later, darling.' And Alex put down the phone.

CHAPTER FIVE

GINNY spent longer preparing for that evening than she'd ever spent in her entire life. Her heart was racing and one moment she was full of nervous excitement and anticipation, the next she felt that she just couldn't go through with it. But in a way Venetia had been impersonating her ever since receiving Alex's letter trying to find her, so why shouldn't Ginny do the same? She told herself that it was also to test her own feelings, to see if what she felt for Alex was real or just an infatuation spurred on by frustration. And perhaps it would test Alex's feelings, too. If he couldn't tell the difference, if he felt the same emotions for her as he did for Venetia... Ginny couldn't think much further than that, was almost afraid to. She had to sit down for a minute as she was getting changed, to still the beating of her heart. There had been so much emphasis, so much suggestion in Alex's voice when he'd implied that they would have the flat to themselves. Had he been waiting for such a moment to take Venetia to bed? Would he—would he want to tonight?

Ginny swallowed, knowing that Venetia would never forgive her if she let him. But then Venetia would probably never forgive her for this anyway. But it was something Ginny had to do, she just *had* to. Or she would feel bitter towards her twin for the rest of her life. And she paid lip-service to her feelings of guilt towards Alex by resolving to tell him the truth after—afterwards.

The phone rang as she was putting on her make-up. Ginny automatically went to answer it but stopped, frozen, just as she was reaching out to pick up the receiver, remembering that she wasn't supposed to be there. Supposing it was some friend of Venetia's, or even Venetia herself, checking up on her. But then again it might be Alex. Darn. Ginny stood irresolute, but the ringing stopped quite quickly. They would have to get an answerphone, she told herself; her nerves couldn't take much more of this.

Going through first her wardrobe and then Venetia's, she dithered for a long time about what to wear, finally choosing a red, figure-hugging sheath dress of her own that was very low at the back. As they swapped clothes all the time it was quite possible that Venetia had worn it on a date with Alex, but Ginny couldn't remember her borrowing it recently. She put her hair up into her most sophisticated style, added black strappy high heels and a little crushed velvet jacket, and was ready a good half-hour too soon. The wait was nerve-racking. Ginny poured herself a gin and tonic and found that her hand was shaking as she held the glass. That wouldn't do; Alex would guess there was something wrong at once.

She tried to steady her nerves by taking a long drink, but still jumped about a foot in the air when the doorbell rang a quarter of an hour earlier than she'd expected. Ginny pressed the button that opened the main door and went out on to the landing to meet him. Alex came bounding up the stairs two at a time, his face lighting when he saw her, his eyes full of eager happiness. At sight of him, knowing that it wasn't for her, Ginny suddenly knew that she couldn't go through with it. The smile left her face, and as he came striding towards her she put up her hands to hold him off, determined to tell him the truth.

But he gave her no time to utter a word as he swept her into his arms and gave her a long, exuberant kiss, a kiss that swiftly deepened into possessive passion.

The world began to whirl round Ginny's head and she felt like Alice in Wonderland, falling and spinning down, down, down into some new, beautiful, and exciting land. But even so, when Alex raised his head at last, she muttered, 'No. Don't.'

He laughed at her, his arms round her, supporting her, which was just as well as her legs seemed somehow to have melted. 'There's no one to see us.'

His eyes were dark with desire, his lower lip—the sexy one—pushed forward. Ginny felt an answering desire rise in her like a great flame and she had to close her eyes for a moment, trying to conquer it. But Alex took it that she wanted him to kiss her again and promptly did so.

'I'm crazy about you,' he murmured unsteadily, his mouth against her neck. 'How much longer are you going to keep me waiting?'

For what, Ginny wondered? Opening her eyes, she looked into his. He doesn't know, she thought. It hasn't even occurred to him that I'm not Venetia. Straightening up, she took his hand and smiled at him. 'I think I'll have to go and redo my make-up before we go out.'

He followed her into the flat. 'Why go out?' he asked, pulling her back into his arms.

Ginny would have given anything to have stayed, to have let that embrace take its natural course, but to her Alex was still virtually a stranger when it came to such intimacy, and she emerged flushed and nervous from his hold. Not like this, she thought, it's all wrong. So she pushed him away, but smiled up at him. 'Hey, give a girl a chance, will you? We have plenty of time.'

'All the time in the world,' Alex agreed. But that didn't stop him from giving her another hungry kiss. 'You're so lovely,' he told her afterwards, his lips tracing tiny kisses along her jawline. 'Have you any idea what being close to you does to me? My beautiful, darling girl.'

Ginny put her arms round his neck and closed her eyes, arching her head back as he kissed her neck. It was so wonderful to hear him say these endearments, bliss. But in her heart she knew they weren't really for her and there was no way she could pretend they were, however hard she tried. She stood still, passive in his arms.

Reluctantly Alex let her go at last, raising his eyebrow in a quizzical look. 'You OK?'

She smiled back. 'Yes, of course. Just hungry.'

He laughed delightedly. 'I should have known. Go and get ready, then, and we'll find somewhere to eat.' Ginny turned to go and Alex gave her a playful pat on the behind as she passed, then laughed again at the startled look she gave him.

Just in time, Ginny remembered to go into Venetia's bedroom and not her own to put on fresh lipstick from her bag. 'How's Jeff?' she called out.

'Fine,' Alex answered. 'Though he's still in a quandary about Ginny.'

As she stood at the mirror, Ginny's hand stilled. 'Oh, why's that?' she asked as casually as she could.

'Well, you know how much he likes her.' Alex came to stand in the doorway, casually leaning against the jamb. 'But he feels that he got off to a bad start with her. He said that she's willing to be friendly, but he's not sure if she really wants him around.'

'Surely she would tell him if she didn't?' Ginny said carefully. 'If Jeff doesn't mind being just a friend——'

'But does he?' Alex interrupted. 'It seems as if he's been pushed into that role whether he likes it or not.'

'I thought he was getting over a broken romance of his own.'

Alex looked puzzled. 'What gives you that idea?'

'Oh, something that Jeff said to—something he said.'

But Alex shook his head. 'That can't be right. Jeff goes out on dates, of course, but he hasn't had a serious affair since he's been at the university, and he's worked there for nearly three years.'

'I must have got it wrong, then.' Picking up a tissue, Ginny carefully blotted her lipstick. She couldn't see Alex directly, only his reflection in the mirror.

'I wish Ginny would fall for Jeff,' he remarked. 'I think they'd be good for each other.' A frowning look came into his eyes for a moment, a look that made Ginny's heart flutter as she wondered whether he was thinking of her, the real Ginny. He must realise that she cared for him; she had dropped a broad enough hint. Broodingly, Alex said, 'And I wouldn't want to be just a friend, if I were him.'

Which could mean anything, good or bad. Wishing that she'd never brought up the subject of Jeff, Ginny gave him a very feminine look under her lashes. 'Ah, but you're biased—or at least I hope so.'

Her distraction worked, because he gave her one of his crinkly-eyed smiles. 'Very definitely,' he assured her. Coming up behind her, he put his hands on her waist, almost encircling it. 'I'll never forget the day I met you; it was the luckiest day of my life.'

Ginny's eyes came up quickly to meet his in the mirror, her eyes full of joy, because now he really was talking about *her*. 'And yet we so nearly lost each other. I really thought you'd stood me up, you know. I thought that probably you were married or something and had changed your mind about meeting me, or else you were just stringing me along.'

'You never told me that before.'

'No—perhaps not.'

'Couldn't you tell that I was the soul of honesty?' Alex complained with a grin.

'Was that what you were? I thought you were just a man trying to pick up a girl.'

'And making a hopeless mess of it,' Alex said ruefully. 'Fancy not asking your name. But it was entirely your fault, you know—you completely bowled me over so that I wasn't thinking straight. I was mad as fire when they wouldn't let me out to meet you.'

'Were you?' Ginny turned to put her arms round his neck, looking up at him in fascinated happiness.

'Of course.' He gave her a lazy smile. 'But you've heard all this before.'

'Tell me again.'

He laughed. 'Well, I tried to argue my way out and when that didn't work I appealed to their sense of romance, telling them that I was in danger of losing the woman who might turn out to be the love of my life. But they have no soul, the French airport officials, and they wouldn't let me go to you.' He spoke lightly, but there was a tenderness in his eyes that caught at Ginny's heart.

'So then?' she prompted.

'So I finally managed to persuade an official to take a note to you, but by then you'd left.'

'I had to,' Ginny said quickly. 'You knew I had to get to the shoot. And I really thought you'd stood me up. But, if it's any comfort to you, I've never waited that long for a man before.'

'Haven't you? Then I'm flattered. You've never told me that before either.'

She flushed a little. 'So what did you do next?'

'Well, I thought of chucking up the conference and scouring Paris for you, but Paris is such a big city that I might never have found you. I didn't know how long you were staying there, you see. So, cursing myself as every kind of a fool for not getting your name, I went to the conference, delivered a very bad speech, and couldn't wait to get back to England so that I could write to all the modelling agencies to try and find you. Luckily I knew your initials, which helped a great deal. But I even bought up a whole pile of fashion magazines and went through them in the hope that your picture might be in one of them. Jeff thought I was turning limp-wristed.'

Ginny laughed delightedly. 'Did you really? How crazy.'

Alex gave her a surprised look. 'But you already know all this.'

'Oh, yes.' Ginny hastily tried to cover her error. 'But I so enjoy hearing it all over again.'

He gave her a warm, tender smile. 'Something to tell your grandchildren?' he suggested softly, nuzzling her neck.

Ginny didn't answer and didn't ask him to go on, knowing that *her* part in the story was over now. From then on it had been Venetia who had stepped into her fairy-tale. She straightened up. 'Let's go, shall we?'

He took her to a bistro restaurant in St John's Wood, a place that Ginny had never been to before, but where Alex had obviously taken Venetia several times, because the proprietor greeted them like old friends. The waiter helped her off with her jacket and they were shown to a table against the wall, a table small enough for them to reach across and hold hands, which Alex did straight away.

'You look absolutely stunning in that dress,' he told her. He smiled, and his hand tightened on hers.

Ginny smiled mistily, knowing that this moment was entirely hers. 'I'm pretty crazy about you, too,' she said sincerely.

The waiter came back again and they had to come down to the mundane level of reading menus and ordering food and wine. 'Let's have champagne,' Alex said impulsively. 'I think that tonight is going to be a very special one.'

Ginny's heart skipped a beat and to cover it she said lightly, 'Does a lecturer's salary run to champagne?'

'Tonight it does,' he said firmly, and gave the order to the waiter.

It hadn't occurred to her to wonder about Alex's financial position before, but he seemed to be OK for money, never sparing any expense when he took Venetia out. And he had paid the bulk of the money for the new car, so he must earn a substantial salary. Ginny didn't like to think about the new car, which had been bought entirely for Venetia's benefit, so, changing the subject, she said, 'I suppose the Easter vacation is coming up for you; how much time do you get off?'

Alex gave her an odd look. 'I told you only last week. We discussed it then, don't you remember?'

'It must have gone out of my mind.' Ginny would have liked to ask him if he'd made any plans for the holiday but was afraid that he might have already discussed it with Venetia.

And it seemed he had, because he leaned forward and said earnestly, 'Why don't you come away with me at Easter? We can go anywhere you like. I have to go to Manchester to take part in a seminar, but apart from that I'm entirely free.'

Ginny stared at him, wondering if this, too, he'd asked Venetia before. And, if so, why hadn't she said yes like a shot? Was she playing hard to get, for heaven's sake? But no, she must be sure of Alex by now. Trying to puzzle it out, Ginny looked into Alex's grey eyes, the flash of desire still in them, and suddenly, intuitively, knew what her twin was playing for. She wanted marriage, nothing less, and was holding herself back until Alex offered it. The knowledge angered Ginny; how could Venetia think herself to be truly in love if she could play that kind of game? OK, marriage to Alex would be wonderful, but to drive him crazy until he was ready to offer it was hardly fair.

Maybe it's my fault, Ginny thought. I was the one who told him that he hardly knew Venetia, and he agreed not to rush her into anything. But maybe she wants to be rushed.

'Hey, remember me?' Alex broke into her train of thought by reaching out and tapping her lightly on the nose. 'You're miles away.'

She wrinkled her nose at him. 'Sorry. I don't really know about Easter, to be honest. We usually go and visit our mother for a few days.'

'But if you could get away—would you come?'

Looking into his face, loving him, Ginny spoke entirely for herself. 'Yes. Anywhere, and for as long as you want.'

'My darling girl.' His face lit and he raised her hand to his lips and kissed it. 'I don't deserve that.'

It was time to bring things down to a saner level. 'Of course you don't,' she agreed, laughing at him. 'Oh, good, here's the food. I'm starving.'

It was a marvellous, wonderful evening, the best that Ginny had ever spent. The only drawback was that she had to be so careful what she said, afraid always of making some remark that would give her away. If Alex were to find out who she was now, it would be disastrous. But thankfully she didn't make any major mistake, and he was so besotted that any slight slips she made were easily glossed over. Alex was very happy, laughing a lot, his attention only for her. Ginny got him to tell her about his life at the university, his family, and his past.

'But you know all this,' he protested.

'Tell me again. I want to know everything about you.'

What man could resist such flattery from a woman he was attracted to? He told her about his parents, who lived in Lancashire where his father was the headmaster of a school. 'And I've written to them and told them about you, by the way,' he told her.

'They want to know when I'm going to take you up there to meet them. Maybe around Easter?' And he raised an eyebrow, but Ginny just smiled. He went on to tell her of his two brothers, one older than him and one younger. The elder brother was also a doctor, but of medicine this time, and worked as a surgeon, again in Lancashire. 'But my younger brother, James, is the brains of the family. He's a scientist, too, and works in the research department of a government-funded company in the United States.'

Hardly the brains of the family, Ginny thought. They all seemed awe-inspiringly clever. 'It must be nice to have a brother,' she remarked. 'I've often thought so.'

'Yes, it's good.' Alex gave her a rather wry look. 'But not such a good idea to have an identical twin, I think.'

Ginny's hand shook, and she had to put down the glass she was holding and put her hands under the table in case he saw. 'Why not?' she said levelly.

'You already know all the reasons.' His voice had become abrupt, but he saw her face and became persuasive. 'You must try to break with Ginny, my darling. It isn't good for the two of you to be so constantly together. Not for you or for her.'

'Or for you, presumably,' Ginny couldn't help remarking tartly.

'That too.' He gave her a steady look. 'Ginny seems to be all mixed-up. I think she'd break us up, if she could. She resents my coming between you, I suppose. Although she said once that she didn't.' He frowned, remembering.

'Perhaps she likes you, too,' Ginny said tentatively, her fingers crossed under the table. 'Perhaps that's why she's so—mixed-up.'

Alex's frown deepened, but he brushed the possibility aside. 'It's hardly likely. No, I think she's just jealous of your interest in me. She's probably afraid of losing you and being left on her own. As you've seldom spent a day apart in your lives it's only natural, unfortunately.'

'I don't think it's unfortunate,' Ginny said shortly. 'It's the kind of relationship that very few people can ever experience. There can be nothing closer than what we share; even a marriage can't be that close. I've never in my life felt lonely because V—because my twin has always been there. And I've never really needed friends.' She groped for words to explain her feelings. 'Sometimes it's as if we're one person. If anything happened to—to my twin then I'd feel as if half of myself had died, too.'

Making an expressive gesture with his hands, Alex said, 'You see what I'm up against. But, darling, you really must try to break away. I know that Ginny has been begging you to give me up, and has been making things difficult for you, insisting that you must go on working together and everything.' Which was a very strong version of the truth. 'It's not as if I'm asking you never to see Ginny again. You can still be——'

'Oh, don't let's talk about it,' Ginny interrupted fiercely. 'Not tonight.'

Alex was immediately contrite. 'You're right. Tonight is special and we don't want to spoil it.'

Spoil it by talking about me, Ginny thought with deep inner anger. She saw now that Venetia had been using her as a pawn in her hard-to-get game with Alex,

embroidering the truth and making her the excuse for
holding back and not giving him what he so desperately wanted. In that moment she decided that Venetia
was going to have a nasty shock waiting for her when
she got home.

'Let's drink a toast,' Alex was saying. He filled their
glasses with champagne and held his up so that the
lights were reflected in it. 'To us, my beautiful darling.'
His voice lowered, became husky.

Ginny clinked her glass against his, her eyes re-
garding him steadily, a warm light of love in their
hazel depths. 'To tonight,' she said softly.

Alex caught his breath, his gaze searching her face,
seeing the assurance there but still unable to believe
it. 'Do you mean it?'

She nodded and drank, but kept her eyes on his.
Then she clinked her glass against his again and
smiled. 'To all our nights.'

'Venetia.' He reached out and took her hand. 'You
don't know how much I want this.'

'Oh, but I do.' Then she blushed under his gaze and
lifted a hand to push back a stray strand of hair.

'There's something different about you tonight,'
Alex remarked, his eyes studying her face. 'But I can't
decide what it is.'

Immediately afraid, Ginny said as lightly as she
could, 'Perhaps it's anticipation and—and nerves, a
little.'

'My sweet.' Capturing her hand, he carried it up to
his lips and kissed her fingers one by one.

He grew impatient, then, to leave, but Ginny took
her time, ordering another coffee and drinking it un-
hurriedly. She wanted tonight to be memorable in
every way; after all, she might only have tonight while

Venetia would have all the time in the world. A problem had occurred to her, too, and one that ought to be faced before they left the restaurant.

'Alex, I—I don't want to go back to the flat.'

He looked surprised. 'But Ginny won't be there.'

'I know, but I don't want to go there,' she said firmly.

Alex looked at her, trying to work it out, but couldn't know that if they went back to the flat he would naturally expect her to take him into Venetia's room, and there was no way Ginny was going to let him make love to her in her sister's bed. He must have reached his own conclusions because he said, 'All right, I'll book us into a hotel. I won't be long.'

He went off to use the phone and came back in about ten minutes. 'I found a hotel not far from here. I told them we were stranded in town so they won't worry about our not having any luggage.'

Ginny nodded, and gave an embarrassed laugh. 'It all feels terribly illicit.'

Alex took her hand. 'It will be very, very wonderful,' he assured her. 'Do you want any more coffee?' She shook her head. 'Then let's go,' he said thickly, unable to keep the vibrant anticipation out of his voice.

It was a beautiful night, the stars so low in the dark velvet of the sky that Ginny felt as if she could reach out and pluck one, hold in her hand the shining radiance of eternity. She stood for a few moments staring up, and Alex said, 'It makes you feel very small in the scheme of things, doesn't it?'

She nodded. 'Very small. Very unimportant. And our problems very—trivial.'

There was a catch in her voice, making Alex put an arm round her. 'Let me take care of your problems.'

There was nothing Ginny would have liked more, but it was impossible. She had gone too far now to tell him the truth. So instead she tried to lighten things by laughing and saying, 'But you are the problem.'

But it had the opposite effect. Catching her shoulders so that she had to face him, Alex said earnestly, 'No, I'm not. This would have happened whoever you'd met. And it could just as easily have been Ginny's problem if she'd met a man first. You only have one life to live, darling. And it's time you started thinking about yourself, about what *you* want.'

'But I am,' Ginny assured him. 'That—that's why I'm here.'

It was impossible for him to understand what she really meant, so Alex took it as he wanted to read it, as a defiant gesture against her twin and as a complete commitment to him. And it was all of that, too, of course. 'My darling girl.' He would have taken her in his arms to kiss her but there were people walking along the street, so instead he tucked her arm in his. 'The car's this way.'

But Ginny hung back. 'Can't we walk? It's such a lovely night.'

'All right.' At that moment he would have given her anything she wanted, done anything she asked. It was a very privileged moment, a time that could come only once in a relationship. And it was Ginny's alone. Whatever happened in the future, Venetia couldn't take this moment away from her, and she would never experience its magic herself. And tonight, although he might never know it, Alex belonged entirely to Ginny, to the girl he had originally fallen in love with.

They didn't hurry, strolling along, their bodies close. And they didn't talk much, content just to be together, knowing that in a short time they would be lovers in every sense of the word. The street was lined with trees, tall plane trees with leaves which were just coming into bud in the warmth of the early spring. It was a well-to-do area, the still-lit shop windows filled with luxury goods. Ginny looked around her, wanting to remember every detail of this night so that she could live it again and again in the years ahead. Her senses seemed to be peculiarly alive, aware of everything around her, sights, smells, the sound of the huge city, the warmth and strength of Alex's hand in hers. But most of all she was aware of the inner tension, the pulsing excitement of her own heart. They came in sight of the hotel and a tremor of nervous anticipation ran through her.

Alex stopped and turned to look at her, ran a finger along her cool cheek. 'Darling. Are you sure?'

She nodded, holding his other hand very tightly. 'Yes,' she said huskily. 'I'm very sure. I'm just—a little chilly, that's all.'

He tried to study her face, but the lights were dim, so presently he turned and they walked on to the hotel. It was large and modern, which Ginny was glad about; she wouldn't have wanted to spend the night in some dingy back-street place. But Alex had chosen well; the hotel was warm and well-furnished, discreetly opulent. The staff, too, were discreet, making no comments about their lack of luggage, and giving them a smiling welcome. They were given the key to Room 225 on the second floor. Ginny looked around the lobby, taking everything in, trying to hold the picture in her mind.

But Alex had eyes only for her, putting his arm round her waist and holding her close to him as they went up in the lift. Ginny could feel the tension in his body, knew that for Alex, too, this would be one of the supreme moments in his life.

The room was larger than most hotel rooms and was dominated by a wide double bed. Ginny saw it as she walked into the room, then turned to Alex. He closed the door on the rest of the world and opened his arms to her. Tossing aside her bag, Ginny ran to him gladly, returning his kiss with an intense ardour that took him by surprise. He gasped, then groaned deep down in his throat as they kissed avidly, hungrily, clinging to each other as passion surged through their veins.

'Oh, God. My darling. My dearest.' Alex rained kisses on her neck, her eyes, along her jawline, and hotly on her mouth again. 'I want you so much, so much.'

'And you. I want you too.' All inhibitions, all pangs of conscience thrown to the winds, Ginny put her hands on either side of his face, kissing him with fierce intensity.

Putting his hands low on her waist, Alex held her against him, letting her feel the growing hardness of his body. It evoked an intense feeling of emptiness deep inside her, making Ginny move her hips against his, filling her heart with a great ache of longing. Alex's breath caught in his throat. He threw back his head, his mouth open in a shuddering groan, his hands gripping her so tightly that it hurt. But she didn't mind, she didn't care. She revelled in this power she had over him, and was overwhelmed by his over her. All the primitive instincts of the ages seemed to fill her veins, driving her mad with desire, with need, with longing. 'Alex.' She said his name on a great sigh of passion.

His hands were trembling as they took hold of hers. Turning them over, he kissed her palms, burying his face first in one hand, then the other. His eyes came up to look at her face, saw the aching hunger in her parted lips, the intensity of her gaze. 'Venetia.' He said the name almost in awe. 'Venetia, my darling.'

Immediately her gaze fell and her mouth closed as she bit her lip.

'Venetia? What is it?'

'Nothing.' Quickly she reached up and kissed him again, shutting off his questions. But there was tension in her body, a touch of desperation in her mouth, until passion claimed them again. Afterwards, her breath unsteady, Ginny reached out and turned down the lights, then, in the dim shadows, said persuasively, 'Alex, you remember when we met on the plane, when we didn't even know each other's name?'

'Mm.' His mouth was tracing a sensuous line down the long, graceful column of her neck while his hands were at her jacket, slipping it from her shoulders.

'Well, if you hadn't been going on to Stockholm we might have——' Ginny gasped as he ran his hands down her bare back, but took a deep breath and went on, 'We might have spent the evening together in Paris and this—this might have happened then.'

'Do you think so?' Alex's voice was hoarse. He had found her zip and was slowly pulling it down.

'Yes. And we—we still might not have exchanged names. We could have been loving strangers.' He didn't answer as he drew her dress off her shoulders and let it slip slowly down her body to the floor, a pool of red on the pale carpet. Putting her hand up to his face, Ginny made him look at her. 'Let's make believe that that's what happened, Alex. That there's been no time in between; that we met on the plane this morning. That we don't even know each other's name.'

'What?' He dragged heavy-lidded eyes away from her slim figure in the delicate lace underwear. 'Make-believe? No, we have no need for that. We have what's real. We have the here and now.'

He tried to pull her into his arms but she held him off. 'Please, Alex. For me.'

He frowned, not understanding. 'But, Venetia, we don't——'

Ginny put her hand over his mouth, looking up at him imploringly, *'Please.'*

For a moment he was still, trying to work it out, but then she came up close to him, let her hips move against his with devastating results. 'All right,' he said hoarsely. 'Whatever you want.'

With a great wave of relief, Ginny abandoned herself to his lovemaking, letting him touch and caress her with his hands and his lips as he slowly undressed her. Then she did the same to him. She took off his jacket first, and then his tie, before reaching up to undo the buttons of his shirt and push it aside to reveal the smooth, strong plane of his chest. Lifting her hands, she let her fingertips run over him, feather-light, feeling the rigidity in his body, feeling the sweat of anticipation on his skin. Circling the hairy areolae of his nipples, she felt the tiny protuberances harden, as sensitive apparently as her own. Alex shuddered, and shuddered again as she bent to kiss them. His skin tasted hot, moist, salty, as she ran her tongue over him. He groaned and guided her hand to his belt. With loving eagerness, she obeyed him.

They didn't go to bed straight away, instead standing together in the dim light, exploring the perfection of each other's body, feasting their eyes on the deliciousness of curves, and feeling the rock-hardness of muscles, the smooth silkiness of skin. Alex took the clips from her hair and watched it flow, rich and silky, down her back. He ran his hands through it, lifted it to his face to smell the clean freshness of it. He cupped her breasts in his hands, kissed them until she cried out, unable to bear the tormenting joy of it, her fingers digging into his shoulders.

But it was when she bent to kiss him that Alex couldn't stand it any longer. He gave a great cry and swept Ginny up into his arms, carried her over to the bed, kissing her passionately as he did so. 'My darling. My little love.' He laid her down on the pillows, his body trembling as he lay down beside her and explored her, telling her how beautiful she was, how much he wanted her.

Alex tried to be gentle with her that first time but was so consumed with desire that he took her in a white heat of passion, making her cry out as her body arched under his. The emptiness deep inside her was filled now, filled with wave after growing wave of pleasure that finally burst on a great surge of ecstasy, as Alex, too, was carried to a surging climax of excitement.

It was over all too soon that first time, and they lay limply clinging to each other, their breathing panting and unsteady, their entwined bodies moist with perspiration.

'My sweet. My darling, beautiful girl.' Alex kissed her face and stroked her hair, his voice, his every panting breath full of wonder and gratitude.

Ginny snuggled closer to him, glorying in his endearments as much as she had gloried in the giving of her body. She was his now, entirely his. She would never love any man as she loved him and never wanted to. And it came perfectly naturally to tell him so. 'I love you,' she said softly, her hand caressing his face. 'I love you so much, my darling.'

His kiss then was deep and tender, the kiss of a man who had found the woman he wanted. But Ginny turned it into passion, exploring his mouth with her tongue and lifting herself to lie over him. His desire for her was far from sated and soon Alex had pulled her down on top of him and was making love to her again, more slowly this time, but with skill, and able to hold back his own climax until he had taught Ginny that she was only on the brink of discovering the pleasure of love.

They made love many times during that night, Alex never seeming to tire of his delight in her. Sometimes Ginny slept, only to be wakened by his kiss or by the sensuous pleasure of his hand gently stroking her. Eventually they both fell asleep but Ginny woke up, disturbed by the weight of Alex's arm lying possessively across her, just as light was beginning to filter into the room. She was facing him and could see the outline of his profile against the whiteness of the pillow. Even in his sleep his mouth was curved, as if he was still remembering with pleasure the wonderful sexual intimacies they had shared. But would it always be like that? Ginny wondered on a sudden surge of guilt. How would Alex look back on this night when she told him the truth?

She had been reaching out to trace the outline of his mouth, half hoping that he would wake and make love to her again, but now she drew back, feeling afraid. Carefully, she slid from under his arm and got out of bed. Alex murmured something in his sleep and turned on to his back but he didn't waken. Their clothes lay scattered on the floor where they had been tossed aside. Ginny picked her way over them and went to the window, opening a small gap in the curtains so that she could look out. It was going to be a beautiful day; low, bright sunshine lay across the garden outside and lit surrounding buildings, turning brickwork and stone to a mellow gold. The first spring flowers, crocuses and daffodils, grew like a carpet of colour across the curve of the lawn. It was the season for love and rebirth and no time to be plagued by pangs of conscience. I just can't tell him, she thought. I know it's cowardly, but I just can't. Not now. Not when it will spoil everything we've shared. Perhaps later I'll tell him what I've done, but not today, not yet.

Pulling the curtains wide, so that the early-morning sun lay across the bed, Ginny walked over and stood beside it. The light disturbed Alex. He blinked and opened his eyes, turned his head to gaze at her. The sun was behind her, creating an aureole of dazzling light rays around her slender body and long, tumbled hair. Alex's eyes widened and he slowly reached out his hand. Ginny put hers into it and for a long moment they clasped hands very tightly, each holding this magic time in their memories. Then Alex drew her down beside him again.

When they woke again it was late and they had to rush so that Alex could get back to Colchester. There was no time for breakfast, and Ginny was rather glad; the night was over now and she didn't want to talk and make plans that she could never keep. Alex went to fetch the car while she dressed, and then he drove her back to the flat. When he pulled up outside they turned to look at each other, knowing that they had both experienced something very special. There were stars of radiance and self-awareness in Ginny's eyes and a new, confident happiness in Alex's face.

Reaching out to take her hand, he said, 'Last night was the most wonderful time of my life. I shall never forget it—or how you looked with the sun behind you this morning. I love you very much, my darling.'

He went to go on but Ginny leaned forward and said softly, 'Don't say any more. Not now.' She kissed him, lingeringly, then got quickly out of the car. 'Goodbye.' Alex pulled away and she waved. 'Goodbye, my love,' she whispered as she gazed after him.

CHAPTER SIX

THE first thing Ginny did when she went into the flat was to take the phone off the hook, then she had a bath and went to bed, falling asleep at once and not waking until late in the afternoon. Even then she didn't get up, but let her mind go back over the previous night, recalling each detail, each moment of love, her mouth curved in a happy smile of remembrance and pleasure. But then her eyes shadowed; the night had been too wonderful, too perfect. She hadn't been able to spoil it by telling Alex the truth as she'd intended. And now it was too late. She could never shatter that wonderful image in his mind by telling him now. By playing her only card to try and win him, Ginny had lost Alex instead.

Venetia would find out, of course—that was inevitable. But Alex would think that he had made love to Venetia, and if her sister had any sense she would let him go on thinking it. Strangely, Ginny felt no stabs of conscience where Venetia was concerned; her twin had taken advantage of her absence to grab Alex, so Ginny had done the same to try and win him back. And she didn't care that she had contrived Venetia's absence. It was all academic now, anyway, because Ginny knew that she had no choice; she must give her sister a clear field.

So, what was *she* going to do? The future lay long and empty before her and right now Ginny didn't much care, but she knew that she couldn't bear to stick around and watch Venetia cement her relationship with Alex. Which meant that she would have to go away somewhere. The only way she could think of to do that was to get a modelling job abroad, in Paris or New York—the latter, preferably, as it was further away. To be good enough to get that kind of job, though, she would need the new portfolio, to get lots of experience, and to become internationally known. It was a tall order but not impossible if one worked really hard. She must concentrate on that and nothing but that. With the thought fixed in her mind, Ginny threw back the duvet and went to shower, wash her hair, and dress.

Putting on her toreador outfit, Ginny strode towards the door, but then remembered the phone and went back to replace the receiver. It began to ring at once. She stared at it, wondering if it could be Alex. It was most probably Alex, she decided, calling to ask how she was, to tell her all over again that he loved her. Her chin thrusting forward, Ginny deliberately ignored the phone and went out of the door.

They were just coming to the end of a shoot at Simon Blake's studio. He was concentrating on what he was doing and didn't notice her at first. As before, Ginny stood out of the way, quietly waiting. She watched him intently, trying to discover what made him so good. She saw how he posed his models, the attention he gave to detail, both of pose and lighting, the way he tossed out an odd sentence of encouragement to put his subject at ease before he became the taciturn photographic artist again. That's what I must do, Ginny thought: give my entire concentration to my work, think about nothing else, let nothing get in its way.

Simon called it a wrap, thanked his models, and made for the door, but stopped when he saw her. 'Hello, Ginny.'

'Hello. I hope you don't mind my coming.'

He shook his head. 'As a matter of fact my secretary has been trying to call you. I've a free morning tomorrow; we could start on your portfolio.' He gave her a speculative look from under thick eyebrows. 'That's if you haven't come to tell me you're no longer interested, of course.'

'The opposite,' Ginny said firmly. 'I very much want to go ahead. And I'd be grateful to learn as much as I can from you. Technique, that kind of thing.'

Simon gave a short laugh. 'Anyone could be a model if all you needed was technique.' He gave her a frowning, almost angry look, then took her arm. 'Come on, let's take a walk.'

He strode along, his hand still on her arm, and took her across Kensington High Street into Kensington Gardens, only then slowing his pace. The park was busy with people walking home from work, briefcases in their hands and tiredness in their eyes, so Simon led her along the Flower Walk until they found an empty bench to sit on.

'Look,' he said to her brusquely. 'I told you before; you're a natural. Trying to deliberately learn how to pose isn't going to make you any better—it might even kill what you've got. So no getting ideas about going to modelling school, OK? You know enough. All you need is experience. And you've got to develop your own personality, your own warmth and vitality, so that it comes across. It will be hard work, of course.'

'That's what I want,' Ginny said shortly, firmly.

Simon didn't ask questions but he must have realised that something had happened to make her so
determined. 'All right. We'll start on the portfolio tomorrow morning. I'll have a make-up expert come to
the studio and a fashion designer friend bring some
of his collection along. If we're going to do this then
it's got to be right.' He raised an eyebrow when she
didn't speak. 'Don't you agree?'

'Absolutely. I'm just—a little overwhelmed by what
you're doing for me.'

He nodded, satisfied. 'Just stay as ambitious as you
are now. I'll get you as much work as I can, and I'll
make sure it's high-class work. And no more ap-
pearances with your twin. That's out from now on,
understand? You're an individual item, Ginny, not
half of a pair.' He looked at her keenly. 'All right?'

He was asking her to do something that had already
happened, Ginny realised. The split had been made
when she had gone behind Venetia's back to be with
Alex last night. She nodded. 'Yes. I understand.'

'Good.' He stood up. 'Come on, the pubs will be
open now. Let's go and talk over a drink.'

The drink led to dinner, so that it was several hours
later before Ginny got back to the flat. There was a
light showing in the glass panel over the door, so she
knew Venetia was home. It took an effort to turn the
key and go in. She had expected Venetia to be full of
rage and to attack her furiously, therefore she was
taken aback when her twin came to the door of her
bedroom and stood there, giving her a strange look.

'Hi,' Ginny said uncertainly. 'How—how did it go?'

'Fine.' Venetia came into the room, her eyes
studying Ginny's face. 'I really enjoyed it. The clothes
were super. There was one girl there who'd worked

with you before, which threw me a bit, but apart from that everything was great.'

'Good, I'm glad.' She doesn't know yet, Ginny realised, and almost wished she did; she couldn't meet her sister's eyes.

'How did your shoot go?' Venetia asked.

Ginny hesitated, realising that now was the time to tell Venetia the truth, but she found that she couldn't bring herself to describe that night with Alex—it was still too precious. So she prevaricated and said, 'Oh. OK.'

'Simon Blake was on it, wasn't he?' Ginny nodded, and Venetia said, 'You must have got home a lot earlier than I did. Have you been out?'

'Yes. With—with Simon, as a matter of fact.'

Venetia's face cleared and Ginny went to turn and go into her room but her twin said hesitantly, 'Did anything happen to you while you were away?'

'What—what do you mean?'

'Did you fall for someone?' Venetia asked bluntly.

Puzzled, Ginny said, 'Why should you think that?'

Venetia gave a thin smile. 'Do you remember saying that you would know if I went to bed with Alex? Well, *I* knew that you went to bed with someone last night. I—I could feel the tension in you. And the excitement and the—the pleasure.' Raising her eyebrows she gave Ginny an almost jealous look. 'It must have been quite a night.'

'Yes. Yes, it was.' Ginny didn't try to deny it. She leaned against the wall, devastated that her twin had been aware of her emotions at such a private time.

'Was it Simon Blake?'

Instead of answering, Ginny went over to the sideboard and picked up an ornament, a pretty ceramic model of a rabbit that had been given to her as a child. Over the years she'd come to think of it as her 'good luck charm'. Holding it in her hands, she turned to Venetia. 'I've got something to tell you. I'm sorry if you don't like it but I've made up my mind.'

Venetia looked at her uneasily. 'You sound very mysterious. This isn't anything to do with Alex, is it?'

'No,' Ginny answered firmly. 'It has nothing to do with him. I've been talking to Simon Blake. He's offered to do a new portfolio for me. But he——'

'He has?' Venetia exclaimed, round-eyed. 'But he charges the earth. How can we possibly afford to pay——?' She broke off, and gave a gasp. 'Good grief, is that why you went to bed with him? Just so he'd do a portfolio for us?' She met a fiery glance of anger from Ginny's eyes and her expression changed. 'Sorry, I know you better than that. You must like him a lot.' But she gave Ginny a puzzled look. 'But you've never really talked about him before.'

'Will you please listen?' Ginny said shortly. Her fingers gripped the rabbit so hard that her knuckles showed white.

'All right. Go ahead, I'm listening.' A note of tension showed in Venetia's voice as she realised that Ginny had something really important to say.

'But you're not. I said that Simon has offered to do a portfolio for *me*. And he's offered to find me work and to—to back me all he can.'

'You?' Venetia said slowly. 'Just you?' And, when Ginny nodded, she said stiffly, 'I see.'

'No, you don't. I tried to tell him that we usually modelled together, but he said we would never get anywhere doing that. He said we have to split up. That we have to do that for one of us to succeed.'

'So why you rather than me?' Venetia demanded on a sulky note. 'I'm just as good as you.'

'I know.' Ginny paused and gave her twin a direct look. 'But you have Alex and I don't.'

There was a heavy silence until Venetia nodded. 'I see.' She turned away, working out the implications. 'So this is where we go our separate ways, is it?'

'That's what you want, isn't it?' Ginny said levelly. 'Now that you've met Alex.'

Venetia went to sit on the sofa, kicking off her shoes and tucking her feet up under her. 'I could still do modelling; I really enjoyed the shoot this week.'

'You want everything, then,' Ginny said tartly.

'No, of course not. OK, I understand that maybe we can't both make the big time, but I don't see why you can't model on your own when work comes along, and we can still do our twin stuff together. That wouldn't be too much to ask, would it?'

'I'm sorry,' Ginny answered reluctantly. 'But Simon insists that if he's going to—to sponsor me then I must go solo from now on.'

'Simon says this, Simon says that! You sound like the party game.' Venetia bounced to her feet. 'And just how am I supposed to live if you go solo and I'm not allowed to model? Has Simon thought of that? Or you, for that matter?'

'We still have the cabaret act,' Ginny pointed out. 'That's if you don't turn down any more engagements because you have a date with Alex.'

Ignoring this thrust, Venetia said angrily, 'I'm not sure if I'm going to agree with all this.'

'It doesn't matter whether you agree or disagree,' Ginny said rather tiredly. 'The decision has already been made. I'm going to Simon's studio tomorrow morning to take the first shots for the portfolio.'

'You might have had the decency to discuss it with me first. Not just thrown it at me as a *fait accompli*.'

'Yes, I might have,' Ginny agreed. 'And ordinarily I would have done, of course. But things aren't very ordinary between us at the moment, are they? We—we've started having secrets from each other,' she pointed out painfully.

Venetia looked at her moodily. She had been pushed into a corner and she knew it. The knowledge that it had stemmed from her own original actions didn't help any. Carefully she said, 'Do I take it that as you're going all out for a modelling career that you have no further—interest in Alex?'

'Do I waive my claim, you mean,' Ginny retorted with a harsh laugh. 'Yes. You could say that.' She gave her twin a keen look. 'Unless you'd rather have the career and I'll have Alex.'

Venetia tossed her head indignantly, her long hair swirling round her. 'Certainly not. *I'm* not mercenary.'

'No, but quite a few other things I could mention.'

Venetia gave her a glaring look. 'I think I'll go and have a bath,' she said shortly.

Ginny carefully replaced the rabbit and went into her own room, firmly closing the door before taking off the toreador suit and putting on jeans and a sweater. She was glad that one secret at least was out in the open. Venetia had taken it very well, considering, but that was only because Ginny had given up her fight for Alex. It was good that it had turned out this way. Now, knowing that Ginny had backed down, Venetia might not be so mad when she found out that she had spent the night with Alex.

Collecting together their clothes that needed washing, Ginny took them out to the kitchen, and began to fill the washing machine, but was interrupted by the phone.

'Hello?'

'Venetia?' It was Alex and for a few seconds she was so overwhelmed to hear his voice that she couldn't speak. Taking her silence for confirmation, Alex said warmly, 'My darling, I've been trying to phone you all afternoon. Did you sleep this morning? I wish I'd been able to after such a wonderfully exhausting night. Or better still, I wish I'd been with you so that we could have gone on making love all day. My darling, did I tell you how much I——?'

'Alex,' Ginny interrupted desperately. 'This is Ginny.'

There was a short shattering silence. 'Why didn't you say so before?' Alex demanded angrily.

'You didn't give me a chance.' Her heart bleeding, Ginny tried to speak normally, but it came out as very cold and stilted. 'I'm afraid Venetia is in the bath. Can I take a message for her?'

'Can't she come to the phone?'

'No, she's locked the door.'

'All right. Will you tell her that I'll come up to see her tomorrow night? But I'm not sure what time I'll be able to make it, so it might be better if I met her at the restaurant around eight o'clock.'

'Which restaurant?'

'The one we went to last night,' Alex replied, his voice warm with the memory.

Knowing that she couldn't possibly tell Venetia that, Ginny racked her brain for the name of the bistro but couldn't remember it. 'What's it called?' she asked faintly.

'She knows it,' Alex answered. Then, thankfully, added, 'Antoine's.'

'I'll tell her,' Ginny said in relief.

'Thanks. I...' Alex hesitated, aware that he had given a great deal away. But, realising that it was too late and there was nothing he could do about it, he said sardonically, 'It might be a good idea to say your name next time you answer the phone, Ginny.' And rang off.

Ginny was watching a film on television when Venetia finally emerged from the bathroom.

'Who was on the phone?' she asked immediately.

'Alex.' Ginny gave her the message.

Venetia's face lit up. 'Good. I've missed him the last couple of days.' She went into the kitchen to get a glass of milk then sat on the sofa, pulling the skirts of her blue bathrobe around her. 'You haven't told me yet what happened last night,' she remarked.

Ginny gave her a sharp look, her face going taut as she tried to conceal her feelings. 'What about last night?'

'Well—was it Simon Blake you went to bed with?'

Slowly Ginny shook her head. 'No, it wasn't Simon.'

Venetia immediately looked intrigued. 'No? Don't tell me you've been seeing someone without telling me? Unless it was Jeff. But it couldn't have been him because I rang Alex last night and Jeff answered the phone. So who——?'

Trying desperately to keep her tone normal, Ginny said, 'You phoned Alex last night?'

'Yes, of course. We ring each other nearly every night, you know that.' Venetia's lips pouted a little. 'But last night he was out, although he didn't say he wasn't going to be at home.'

'Did—did Jeff tell you where he'd gone?'

'Some last-minute meeting or other.' Venetia shrugged. 'Don't try to change the subject. If it wasn't Simon or Jeff, who were you with last night? Surely it couldn't have been someone you met on the shoot? Good heavens, that was fast work. And not a bit like you. Only a few days ago you were still mooning after Alex.' Her eyes narrowed and she spoke slowly, putting her thoughts into words. 'Unless it was because you couldn't have Alex and so you just went to bed with the first available man who came along.' She gazed at Ginny, aghast. 'Oh, God, you didn't, did you?' She stopped, staring into Ginny's face.

'You must be tired,' Ginny said, turning away to look at the television again. 'Why don't you go to bed?'

But Venetia wasn't to be put off so easily. 'That was a crazy thing to do. Going to bed with some man you hardly know. How could you possibly do it? You must have been mad.'

'Yes,' Ginny agreed. 'I rather think I was.'

Venetia stared at her, unable to penetrate the wall of coolness Ginny had put between them. 'I can't believe that you'd do a thing like that. You're just not—not that type.' Ginny didn't answer, and Venetia shook her head in amazement. 'To go with a stranger, just because you couldn't have Alex. That's a terrible thing to do. And what a risk you were taking. You do realise that, don't you?'

'I realise everything,' Ginny answered shortly.

Annoyed, Venetia came right out with it and said, 'Who is this man?'

Without looking at her, Ginny said drily, 'Venetia—go to bed.'

Realising that she wasn't going to get any more out of her, Venetia gave Ginny a baffled look and got to her feet. 'All right, don't tell me, then. But don't think I won't find out.' And she went to her room, slamming the door behind her.

Ginny gazed at the closed door, wryly thinking that Venetia was going to find out a lot sooner than she expected.

The next morning Ginny got up to go jogging as usual before changing and going on to Simon Blake's studio, arriving much too early and having to wait on the doorstep until he turned up. He was pleased by her promptness, though, and they got straight down to work. Because of the time it took to try on the clothes, do her make-up, and put her hair into different styles, they only took Ginny in three outfits that morning, although Simon shot rolls of film.

'Good,' he said approvingly when they'd finished. 'This should give us three studies for your portfolio.'

And a good portfolio could have as many as ten photos. Ginny tried to work out the cost and felt faint at the result. Mega-expensive. It would take her *years* to pay Simon back. Simon was having lunch with a client and had to hurry off, leaving Ginny to use the shower in the dressing-room at the studio before going to a salad bar for lunch followed by a prolonged stroll round the shops to buy tights and some new make-up. Prolonged because she didn't want to go home. But it had to be faced some time. Jumping on a bus, Ginny made her slow way back to the flat.

Venetia was in the kitchen, making some yoghurt. 'Hi. How did it go?'

'Fine. We did three shots.' Ginny looked at her sister in surprise, not having expected her to be this cheerful.

'Are you hungry? I could make you something.'

'Thanks, but I ate at lunchtime.' She gave Venetia a wary look. 'You seem very happy.'

'Of course I am; I'm seeing Alex. Here, have a strawberry; there's some left.'

For a few minutes they stood eating the strawberries and it was like old times, as it had been for all the years of their lives, being together, sharing things. They looked at each other and smiled tentatively. But then Ginny looked away, the fruit in her mouth suddenly tasting like sawdust, when she realised that this companionship would end forever when Venetia found out that she'd spent a night with Alex. I shouldn't have done it, she thought, I should have had the strength to walk away and leave them to their romance. But she hadn't had the will-power—and nor had Venetia, if it came to that. And Ginny was fiercely glad that she had that one night to treasure.

'Ginny,' Venetia said on the kind of note that meant she wanted something, 'I've been thinking. About what you said last night. You know, when Simon Blake said that only one of us can succeed in modelling. Well, I think he's right.'

'Of course he is. I think deep down we both knew it, we just couldn't bring ourselves to face it, though. Because we've always done everything together and we——'

'Yes, I know all that,' Venetia said impatiently. A gleam came into her eyes. 'But what's to stop us both getting work from the same portfolio? We could do as we did this week; you could take one assignment and I could take another.'

'But that wouldn't be right.'

'Why not? The clients would still be getting the model they asked for. And that way we could both get work. I'd have to join another agency of course, but we——'

'We can't,' Ginny broke in vehemently. 'We just can't.'

'I don't see why not. We've done it once already.'

It was impossible to tell Venetia that they hadn't, that Ginny had not gone on an assignment at all. 'We just can't, that's all. It wouldn't be fair on Simon for a start. And it would be bound to be found out and then neither of us would ever get any more work.' She held up her hands as Venetia looked as if she was going to argue. 'I'm not going to do it, Venetia, and that's final.'

'Not necessarily,' Venetia said shortly. 'Just because you've decided to go it alone doesn't stop me from doing the same. I could have a new portfolio done for myself, and then we'd see which of us became successful.'

'Neither of us, most probably. The result would be the same. But if you want to do that, then it's your privilege, of course.'

'You realise this is emotional blackmail?' And, when Ginny didn't answer, Venetia said persuasively, 'Will you let me have copies of Simon Blake's photographs for my portfolio?'

Ginny gave her a hard look. 'You already know the answer to that one.'

'I don't see why. We've always shared everything before. And we've been taking each other's place all our lives. Why shouldn't we go on doing it?'

Knowing that she'd taken Venetia's place one time too many, Ginny said heavily, 'You know why.'

Her twin's lips pouted into a moue of disappointment. 'I was afraid you'd say that. Although it wouldn't have hurt you to do it at least until Alex and I—well, until something comes of it.'

'You'll marry him, then, if he asks you?' Ginny asked painfully.

Venetia gave her a confident smile, enjoying getting her own back. 'He *will* ask me, and yes, I will marry him.'

She went to get ready to go out soon afterwards but around seven the phone rang. Ginny was standing by it and picked up the receiver. 'Hello?'

'Who is that?' Alex's voice answered and her knees began to tremble.

'It—it's Ginny.'

'Forgotten already?' His voice was cool, almost curt. 'I'd like to speak to Venetia.'

'H-hold on.' Ginny put the receiver down carefully, fighting an overwhelming urge to cut him off and leave the phone off the hook. But Venetia would have heard it ring. Going to her sister's door, Ginny called, 'It's for you. Alex.'

'OK, I'm coming.'

And now she was bound to find out the truth. Going over to the window, Ginny stood looking out through the frilled net, but not seeing anything, her ears straining to hear what was said.

'Hello, Alex, darling. You're on your way! How marvellous. Mm, I'd love to go to a film. There's a new one at the Odeon, Leicester Square, I'd like to see.' She listened for a few moments. 'Tuesday night? The night before last. But I was...' The puzzlement in her voice faded as she went on listening. To endearments, Ginny realised, to words of love, to the knowledge that her sister had stolen her place in Alex's bed. 'Yes,' Venetia said hollowly. 'It was for me, too. A—a wonderful night.'

Slowly Ginny turned to face her sister, her own features a set, expressionless mask.

Venetia gave her a look of searing, scorching fury and spoke into the phone. 'Alex, I'm sorry, I'll have to go. Ginny has just come in. Yes, you too, my darling. See—see you shortly. Goodbye.' She put the phone down very carefully, as if it were of delicate porcelain, then erupted into movement, throwing herself across the room and hitting out at Ginny with furious hate-filled eyes. 'You pig! You rotten cow.' She clawed her hands to try to scratch Ginny's face, but, when Ginny put her arm up to defend herself, grabbed hold of her hair instead, giving it a vicious tug, trying to tear it out by the roots.

Ginny had intended to just stand there and take whatever Venetia did to her, because she felt that she deserved it, but the pain soon put paid to any stoicism and she was filled with a glorious sense of outrage. 'It's your own fault,' she yelled at Venetia. 'You shouldn't have stolen him from me in the first place.'

But Venetia was too enraged to listen. 'You bitch!' She swung her arm with her full force, catching Ginny on the side of the jaw and sending her flying.

Dazed, Ginny struggled to get up, but Venetia launched herself at her, pushing her back on the floor and first pummelling at Ginny with her fists, then trying to rake her face with her nails. They rolled on the floor, equal in size and strength and equally enraged. Ornaments tumbled as they crashed against a coffee-table and the sideboard. A pedestal lamp came smashing down and a vase of daffodils fell, narrowly missing Venetia, the water making a dark stain on the carpet. But the next minute the flowers were crushed as the girls rolled over them, Venetia still cursing furiously and trying to hurt, and Ginny trying to ward her off.

They must have been fighting for several minutes before Ginny's anger suddenly evaporated and she realised how stupid and futile it was. 'Venetia, stop it. There's nothing to fight about.' But her twin took no notice and landed her a blow in the ribs. 'Ouch! Listen to me, will you?' Putting her feet against the wall, Ginny braced herself and, getting her hands against Venetia's shoulders, managed to throw her off. 'Now listen. I——' She broke off, ducking, as her twin picked up all the fallen ornaments she could reach and flung them at her. They hit the wall, shattering into pieces. One of them was her lucky charm rabbit.

Slowly Ginny reached out and picked up the largest fragments, her face drawn. 'You didn't have to do that.'

'Serves you damn well right,' Venetia said viciously.

They leaned against the walls at opposite sides of the room, as if they were boxers resting after the bell had gone. Their breathing was ragged and unsteady and they eyed one another warily, ready to start fighting or defending again at the slightest sign of aggressiveness. Venetia was wearing a housecoat over her underwear; it had come open and one of the sleeves was almost torn off, while Ginny had a red mark on her jaw and there was thin trail of blood running from a deep scratch near her temple.

Ginny could feel the waves of hate and anger coming from her twin but herself felt only despair. 'Do you realise what we're doing?' she said unsteadily. 'We're fighting each other—and all over a man.'

'It's not just a man—it's Alex. And you—you've been to bed with him!' And Venetia burst into tears.

After letting her cry her anger out for several minutes, Ginny said, 'You don't have anything to cry about; I won't try to take him away from you any more.'

'What—what do you mean?' her twin asked between sobs.

'What I said. I'm going to concentrate on modelling from now on. Alex is all yours.'

Venetia stopped crying to stare at her. 'You don't mean it,' she said suspiciously. 'It's just a cheap trick.'

'No. Not any more.'

'Why?'

'We can't both have him. I was a fool to hope that I could get him back after Alex had got to know you and fallen in love with you,' Ginny admitted honestly.

'So why did you go to bed with him?' Venetia demanded. 'Just for spite, I suppose.'

Ginny gave a tired sigh. 'I only intended to go out with him. I wanted to prove to him that he could mix us up, that even his feelings were the same for both of us, and at the end of the evening I was going to tell him that I was the one he'd met originally. But then one thing led to another and I found myself going to bed with him.' She paused then slowly shook her head, her mouth twisting bitterly. 'But no, that isn't true, even though I try and tell myself it is. I think I subconsciously hoped all along that the evening would turn out the way it did.'

Venetia stared at her, still not convinced. 'Do you swear that you're going to keep away from him?'

'Cross my heart and hope to die.' Ginny crossed her chest as she said it, remembering the countless times they'd used the same promise in childhood.

But Venetia was still grim. 'It was a dirty trick to play.'

'Yes, I know. I'm sorry.'

'Was it—was it wonderful?'

'Yes,' Ginny answered sincerely. 'It was a night I shall never forget.'

'Then I don't understand; why are you willing now to give him up?'

Ginny sighed again. 'First, because it was such a magical night that I couldn't spoil it by telling Alex that I'd deceived him.'

'And second?' Venetia prompted when she didn't go on.

'Second? Because I'm beginning to think that Alex is too good for either of us. He doesn't deserve to be deceived the way we've deceived him. As far as he's concerned he's fallen for one girl and that's the way it ought to be.' She gave her twin a brooding look. 'We both love him—nothing can change that—but it's about time we stopped being selfish and thought of Alex.'

Venetia stared at her in growing wonder. 'So you're going to back off?'

'Yes. That's why I'm having the new portfolio done; so that I can concentrate on modelling and hopefully go and live and work abroad as soon as possible.'

'Leave England? Leave—me?' Her twin gave her a disturbed look.

'Yes.'

'But we've never been parted for more than a few weeks in all of our lives. How could I be happy if you weren't around?'

'You'll have Alex to make you happy,' Ginny pointed out on an acid note.

'You don't *have* to go abroad. You could stay in England.'

Ginny shook her head, wincing because she must have banged it when she fell. 'No,' she said firmly. 'I'm not strong enough to stay here and see you and Alex together. Not after the night I spent with him.'

'Is he—is he a good lover?' Venetia blurted out, unable to resist.

'I expect you'll find out.' Ginny's face grew grim. 'At least now you'll have no excuse to go on playing cat and mouse with him.'

Venetia's cheeks coloured. 'I want to marry him; is there anything wrong in that?'

'No, so long as you don't drive the poor guy mad with frustration or make an ultimatum out of it: marriage or nothing. Alex deserves better than that.'

'So you keep saying,' Venetia said on a sulky note. 'But he kept talking about taking our time and being sure of our feelings; I thought he wanted us to just live together.'

'What's so wrong with that? At least you'd be sure——'

'But I *am* sure,' Venetia burst out. 'I'm crazy about him—and I don't want anything less than marriage.'

Ginny stared at her. 'Maybe you love him more than I do, then. Because I'd be willing to settle for anything he cared to give me.'

Venetia found no answer to that. They were silent for a while, sitting on the floor in the battleground that the room had become until Venetia said, 'Well, at least we know where we stand now.'

'Yes.' A thought occurred to Ginny. 'But no using me as an excuse to hold Alex off any more.'

'How can I hold him off now?' Her face desolate, Venetia said, 'You've cheated me out of my wedding night with Alex.'

'You've cheated me out of a whole lifetime with him,' Ginny returned shortly.

They gazed at each other, assimilating the knowledge that nothing was ever going to be the same between them again. Into the silence came the sound of a key turning in the lock and Alex walked into the room. He stopped in the doorway, staring at the girls, at the room.

'Dear God, what's happened?' He looked from one to the other of them uncertainly. 'Venetia?' But they were both held silent, waiting to see which one of them he would go to. Fear making him angry, Alex burst out, 'For God's sake, one of you say something!'

'Alex.' Venetia held out her arms.

Quickly he went down on his knees beside her. 'What the hell's happened here? Are you hurt?' He took Venetia gently into his arms. 'Did someone break in, attack you?'

That's what it must look like, Ginny realised, glancing round the wrecked room. Her eyes went back to Alex; there was such an expression of worried tenderness on his face as he held Venetia that it physically hurt to see it. Scrambling to her feet, Ginny said shortly. 'No, it was a private fight.'

'What!' He stared up at her disbelievingly. 'You mean the two of you . . .'

He turned back to Venetia, but she very wisely said, 'Oh, Alex,' and buried her face in his shoulder as she burst into tears.

'What have you done to her?' Alex demanded, glaring at Ginny.

She gave a small, bitter smile at that and, turning away, picked up the lamp and set it back on its base. It gave her a few seconds in which to decide what to do, then, her mind made up, she faced him again. Lifting her chin, Ginny said clearly, 'We had a row. I told Venetia that I didn't want to model with her any more. I've found a sponsor and I'm going it alone. I also told her to keep out of modelling from now on.' Venetia had stopped sobbing and was staring at her, open-mouthed. 'She didn't go much on the idea,' Ginny added caustically.

Alex gave her a grim look. 'Which is hardly surprising. But did you have to hit her when she argued with you?'

'Oh, no, really. It was my fault, too. I——'

But Alex wouldn't listen to Venetia's mumbled intervention. 'I'm quite sure it wasn't.' Bracing his shoulders, he picked Venetia up and carried her, clinging round his neck, into her bedroom.

He was gone for some little time and Ginny could imagine how he was comforting her twin, kissing her, murmuring words of encouragement and endearment, perhaps bathing her face. Again Ginny felt that terrible stab of grief and desolation. She wanted to run out of the flat and keep on running until her strength gave out, then just lie on the ground and fall into oblivion, never waking up. She didn't know how she was going to face living without Alex, without even the hope of his loving her. Instead she methodically began to clean up the sitting-room and had almost finished when he came out of Venetia's room.

'I want a word with you,' he said shortly, and, taking her arm in a firm grip, pulled her into the kitchen and shut the door. His eyes were blazing angrily, as full of deep emotion as they had been on that night they'd made love. But what a different emotion now. 'You spiteful little cat!' he said furiously. 'You just can't bear to have Venetia loving someone other than you, can you? You want her all to yourself. To go on as you've always done.' He was still holding her arm and shook her in the intensity of his anger. 'But you're a fool to yourself, Ginny, because now you've really lost her. I love Venetia and I'm going to marry her. As her sister you would have been welcome in our home, but now I'm going to make sure that she sees as little of you as possible.' He shook her again, gritting his teeth in scarcely controlled fury. 'Do you understand?'

'Yes, you make yourself very clear,' Ginny answered with the calmness that came of numbed desolation.

But Alex hardly listened. 'I've been as patient with you as I know how, for Venetia's sake, but I'm sick to death of your insane, unnatural jealousy. And this last trick, to deprive Venetia of a means of earning her living, is despicable. And the poor girl's actually been forgiving enough to agree to it, too. She says that it's only fair.' Alex shook his head in wonderment. 'How she can be so unresentful after all you've done to her I fail to see. And how two sisters can look so much alike and yet be so different in temperament, one so gentle, the other so vicious...' Words failed him.

Ginny looked steadily into his eyes, her own bleak, trying to ignore his words because he didn't understand, but feeling them like the cuts of a knife.

Mistaking her calmness for stolid defiance, Alex said in a burst of fury, 'Just keep away from us in future. Venetia doesn't want you. I'm her life now— not you!'

CHAPTER SEVEN

GINNY stayed in the kitchen until she heard Alex and Venetia go out, the front door slamming behind them. Only then did she relax the tension that had held her rigidly standing at the sink, gripping its edge. Somehow she managed to let go and stumble into her own room, throwing herself down on the bed. She began to cry, soft little moans of despair that soon became convulsive sobs. Dimly she heard the phone ringing in the sitting-room, but let it ring, not caring who it was. It stopped but rang again half an hour later, and went on ringing at half-hourly intervals for a couple of hours. There was silence, then, but there wasn't any peace in her mind. Too heartbroken even to think about the future, Ginny wrapped her arms round herself in an agony of despair and cried for the love that she'd not only lost but given up.

It must have been around ten o'clock when someone pressed the doorbell. Ginny heard it but ignored it. But whoever was there simply put a finger on the bell and held it there. It was a loud, shrill bell that set her teeth on edge and made her cover her ears, but Ginny couldn't shut it out. Neither could she shut out the bangs on the door and the sound of a masculine voice calling her name.

'Oh, hell!' Exasperated beyond endurance, Ginny rolled off the bed and strode angrily into the sitting-room, yanking open the front door. 'What the hell do you want?' she demanded violently.

Taking his finger off the bell, Jeff's eyes went swiftly to her face, taking in the tear-swollen eyes, the cut on her temple and livid swelling on her jaw. Quickly he pushed her inside, away from the curious neighbours who'd come out of their flats to see what was happening.

'What are you doing here?' Ginny said shortly, still angry.

Jeff pushed the door shut and looked around. Although the room was tidy there was still a stain on the carpet and a complete absence of ornaments to tell him that something had happened. 'I was worried about you. You didn't answer the phone so I decided to come up here.'

'I could have been out,' Ginny retorted.

'Your light was on. And you weren't out, were you?' Taking her arm, Jeff led her to the centre of the room under the light and took a closer look at her face. 'That's going to be quite a bruise.'

Pulling her arm free, Ginny put a hand up to her face. Her jaw hurt when she touched it. 'What do you want?' she asked ungraciously.

Jeff eyed her carefully, wondering what to say, then, 'You duped Alex into spending the night with you on Tuesday. I know because Venetia called him that night and obviously knew nothing about the date she was supposed to have with him.' He paused, waiting for Ginny to speak, but she just turned away. 'I knew that he was bound to find out the truth tonight, and I was going to ask him to bring me up here with him so that I could give you some support. I waited for him at home, but when he didn't show up I realised he must have gone up to town direct from his meeting. So I tried to call and find out what had happened.'

Going over to the drinks cupboard, Ginny took out
the gin and poured two glasses. 'You needn't have
come,' she said shortly as she gave one to Jeff. 'It's
all over. Finished.'

He eyed her narrowly. 'Was it Alex who hit you?'

She gave a short laugh. 'No, that was Venetia. Alex
doesn't hit out with his fists, only with words.'

'But maybe he's entitled to after the trick you played
on him.'

Ginny frowned, then realised that Jeff had got it
all wrong. 'You don't understand; Venetia found out
the truth when Alex spoke to her on the phone this
evening. By the time Alex got here it was all over and
I'd—my sister and I had decided on our future.'

'But Alex must still have been furious when Venetia
told him.'

'We didn't tell him,' Ginny admitted baldly. She
gave Jeff a look of fierce determination and gripped
the hand that held his drink so violently that the liquid
spilled and he winced in sudden pain as her nails dug
in. 'And nor must you.'

'But he *has* to know. You can't just——'

'No, he doesn't. Can't you see? If he finds out he'll
never trust either of us again. At least let one of us
be happy with him.'

'And that one is going to be Venetia?'

'Yes.' Ginny's eyes shadowed, grew bleak, but then
settled on him fiercely again. 'You must swear not to
tell him, Jeff.'

'But, Ginny...' Jeff made a helpless gesture. 'He's
my closest friend. I can't deceive him like this.'

'You will if you're really his friend. And anyway,
you already have, haven't you? You've known the
truth for two days and you haven't said anything to

him. You even connived at it by covering for me when
you spoke to Venetia.'

'Yes, I suppose I did,' Jeff admitted heavily. He
shook his head. 'But to keep something like that from
him . . .'

'But you'll do it?' she pressed. 'You must promise.
For Alex's sake, Jeff.'

He gave her a direct look. 'Perhaps, although I'm
not so sure about that. But I will do it because you
ask me to.'

She searched his face, looking for the reassurance
that he would keep his word, then she let him go and,
turning away, went over to the window and leaned
against the wall, looking out at the spreading lights
of the city. 'Why *did* you cover for me?' she asked.

Reaching up, Jeff took off his glasses and began to
polish them on a handkerchief. 'I don't know, really.
I suppose because I thought it might be a good idea
for you to go out with him and have a chance to get
to know him better. You might even have found that
you weren't keen on him, after all. But when he didn't
come home that night . . .' Jeff's voice grew ragged,
making Ginny turn and look at him. Without his
glasses he looked very young and vulnerable, a completely different man. 'Then I cursed myself for every
kind of a fool because I knew it could only lead to
terrible trouble for all three of you.' He hesitated,
adding slowly, 'And I knew that it meant that I'd lost
any chance I had with you.'

Ginny didn't attempt to deny it, simply saying, 'I'm
sorry.'

He nodded, and replaced his glasses, hiding his
feelings behind them, becoming detached again. 'Is
there anything I can do for you?'

'No thanks.' She gave him a sad look. 'It was kind of you to drive all this way.'

'That's what friends are for, aren't they?' he said with a shrug. 'We did say that we'd have a go at being friends.'

'But it's not what you really want, and I'm sorry, but I have nothing more to give.' And Ginny spread her hands in an empty gesture.

'OK.' Jeff straightened his shoulders, finished his drink in one swallow and set down the glass. 'But I'd like to know how you're getting along. And I don't suppose Alex will tell me after tonight. So can I call you now and again?'

'Of course.' She went over to him and put her hand over his, able to feel compassion for him even through her own heartbreak. 'As often as you like. And—and look me up if you're ever at a loose end in London.'

'Of course.' But they both knew that he wouldn't. Jeff lifted his hand and gently ran it down her face. 'You're one of the bravest women I've ever met, Ginny. Don't let this throw you.' He gave a crooked kind of smile. 'They say that time heals everything. I think we're about to find out.' Leaning forward, he kissed her on the mouth, a kiss in which he drank in the sweetness of her lips, her youth, and her beauty. A kiss that he would remember and treasure always. Then he dragged his mouth away, abruptly turned and strode out of the flat.

Slowly Ginny closed the door after him then went into her room and went to bed.

Venetia didn't come home until gone midnight. Lying awake, Ginny heard Alex's voice as they said goodnight, but he didn't come in. As soon as he'd gone Venetia came to tap on her door but Ginny didn't answer, pretending to be asleep. Whether Venetia was fooled or not she didn't much care; there was no way that she wanted to discuss the events of the evening with her twin tonight.

When Ginny looked into the mirror the next morning she knew that there was no way she was going to be able to work for at least a couple of days. Her eyes were swollen, and dark-lined with tiredness, and the mark on her jaw had turned a beautiful blue and purple. She could probably cover the bruise with make-up, but nothing was going to disguise her eyes. But luckily it was nearly the weekend and they had no cabaret engagements, so it didn't matter too much. Ginny balled her hands into tight fists, not wanting to face Venetia, not wanting to go on as if nothing had happened. Coming to a swift decision, she threw some clothes into a bag and left a note for her twin on the fridge, saying that she was spending the weekend with a friend, adding, 'Don't worry about Jeff. I've spoken to him and he's promised not to say anything to Alex.' Hoping that this would go some little way towards atoning for what she'd done to Venetia, Ginny then let herself out of the flat, picked up the car and headed out of London.

Taking the first motorway that she came to, Ginny headed north but turned off at Newmarket when she saw a sign for the races. She liked horses and was in the mood to get lost in a crowd. Because it was still early in the day she was able to find a parking space and went into the race-course as soon as it opened. Finding a place near the track, she leaned her arms on the rail to watch. It was a beautiful spring day, much too warm for the time of year. The sort of day that it was fashionable for her generation to blame on the greenhouse effect, her parents on the atom bomb, and her grandparents to thank God for. The horses were beautiful, so strong and sleek, magnificent in their breeding and confidence. With a total disregard for money, Ginny placed several bets and actually won twice, one of them being on a twenty-to-one outsider that she'd backed because she'd liked the horse's colour and the way he pricked his ears. Invigorated by her win and the excitement of watching the horses thunder by, Ginny looked at her race card to choose a horse for the fifth race. One of them was called Alex's Choice. Suddenly everything turned to dust and ashes and she dropped the card, turning blindly away and pushing through the crowd, the gap where she had stood immediately filling as if she'd never been there.

Ginny spent that night and the next at bed and breakfast places somewhere along the road, Saturday walking round the crowded city of Norwich and the whole of Sunday sitting in the car in a car park, just waiting for the hours to pass. She wondered if Alex would use the opportunity of her absence to go to bed with Venetia, but, when the nights had passed, knew they hadn't; she was so emotionally close to her twin that she would have been aware of it if they had, just as Venetia had been with her. It was going to be difficult for Venetia when they did go to bed together, Ginny realised. Alex would think it was the second time for her and her twin would have to try and pretend it was so, might even have to stifle some of her own emotions to make Alex believe it. Ginny was sorry now if she'd made it hard for her sister, but there was no way she was sorry about spending the night with Alex.

It was very late when Ginny got home on Sunday night; she'd fallen asleep in the parked car, and then taken a wrong turning and got lost. But Venetia was waiting up for her and got quickly to her feet when Ginny came in. She looked at her anxiously. 'Are you all right? I've been worried about you.'

'Yes, of course. Fine.' Ginny carried her bag into her bedroom and would have shut the door but Venetia came in after her.

'Where have you been?'

'Didn't you see my note? I've been staying with a friend. I had a marvellous time; we went to Newmarket races and I won over a hundred pounds. I haven't spent any of it; you can have some, if you like.'

But Venetia didn't believe her and wouldn't be side-tracked. 'Ginny, we have to talk.'

'Of course, but not now, OK? I'm tired.'

'But I waited up for you.'

'You shouldn't have done that.'

Pulling her nightdress from her case, Ginny went to go to the bathroom, but Venetia barred her way. There was a worried frown on her face and she reached out and caught hold of Ginny's arm. 'I was so worried about you; I thought you were going to do something crazy.'

Ginny shook her head and touched Venetia's hand. 'No, you should have known I'd never do anything like that.'

'I think I might have done if it had been the other way round.'

'No, you wouldn't.' Ginny sighed. 'Look, I'm back home safe and there's nothing to worry about. Why don't you go to bed and let me——?'

'But I need to talk to you,' Venetia insisted.

'There's nothing to talk about; it's all decided. I'm going to be an internationally famous model and you're going to marry Alex and be a bored housewife.'

She went to go past Venetia but her twin said, 'That's what I wanted to talk to you about. I wanted to tell you before anyone else. Alex and I....' Venetia paused but couldn't keep the elation out of her voice. 'We're engaged. He asked me to marry him.'

Ginny had reached out to open the door. She gripped the handle hard, trying to stop the pain showing in her face. She'd been expecting this, hadn't she? she told herself fiercely. Alex had already told her that he wanted to marry Venetia. So why then did it hurt so much?

'Congratulations,' she managed to mumble. 'When did he ask you?'

'Well, actually...' Venetia hesitated.

Ginny gave a harsh laugh of understanding. 'It was on that night we fought, wasn't it?'

Venetia nodded unhappily. 'I'm sorry, Ginny.'

'I don't want your pity,' Ginny shot out, turning on her fiercely. 'You've got what you wanted, what you were holding out for. Now just be happy—and make darn sure that you make Alex happy, too.' And she jerked open the door and went into the bathroom.

The girls didn't see very much of each other during the next couple of weeks. Venetia got herself a temporary office job to earn money for her trousseau while Ginny went for more photo sessions for her portfolio and spent most of her time when she wasn't working either at the agency or at Simon's studio. His secretary was away with the flu so she helped out at the reception desk.

'I've a present for you,' Simon told her one evening when everyone else had gone. 'Come and take a look.' He led her over to the large table he used to lay out photographs and picked up a folder. Opening it, he took out a sheaf of photographs and spread them out. 'Your new portfolio,' he said with a touch of pride.

The photos were far better than Ginny had dared to hope. They caught her in a dozen moods, from romping tomboy to ethereally cool. In latest with-it street fashion and sophisticated evening wear. But in all of them Simon had made her look exquisitely beautiful. Ginny gave a gasp of awed pleasure when she saw them. 'Oh, Simon. They—they're just marvellous. You've made me look far better than I am.'

'Make-up artists and hairdressers can do wonders,' he agreed. Then grinned. 'But it helps if the basics are already there.'

Ginny laughed, glad that he was so matter-of-fact. 'I can't thank you enough, Simon.' And she bent to look through the photographs again.

'Well, it's nice to hear you laugh. You haven't been doing it much lately.'

Her face shadowed, but Ginny didn't look up. 'I'll take the portfolio along to the agency first thing tomorrow. They'll be so pleased with it. And it's bound to bring me more work.'

'It already has,' Simon remarked, accepting her change of subject. 'I showed it to a friend of mine who happens to be the head of an advertising agency. They're looking for a girl to take part in an advertising campaign for a new line of cosmetics—and you've got the job.'

'Without their even seeing me?' Ginny stared at him in astonishment. 'But that's almost unheard of.'

'Well, I did put in a good word for you.'

'Oh, Simon.' Impulsively Ginny threw her arms round his neck and kissed him. 'This is—this is fantastic.'

Putting his arm round her waist, Simon returned the kiss but let her go when he felt her stiffen. 'It will be hard work, mind,' he warned her. 'They want you not only for the photo sessions but to take part in the publicity campaign as well. Go to launch days in countries all over Europe; that kind of thing. I told them you were free to go—is that right?'

'Yes. Definitely. In fact I'd—I'd be quite pleased to get away for a while,' Ginny admitted.

'Good. It's an up-market perfume, so they want to photograph you against those kind of backgrounds: stately homes, a ball, Wimbledon, Ascot.'

Ginny smiled inwardly, thinking of her day spent leaning on the rail among the crowd at Newmarket races; somehow she didn't think Simon's friends had the same thing in mind. Looking up at him, she said sincerely, 'I won't let you down, Simon. I'll work really hard.'

He nodded approvingly. 'I'll tell the agency and get the contracts signed up. They want you to start after Easter.'

That evening they went out to dinner to celebrate, Ginny insisting that it was her treat, which Simon only agreed to after she'd told him about her win at the races. 'I like racing, too. We'll go some time,' he told her, making it a definite fact rather than an invitation.

Venetia was still up when Ginny got in. She was watching television but immediately turned off the set.

'Hello.' Venetia gave a sleepy yawn. 'Had a good evening?'

'Yes. Dinner with Simon.' Ginny hesitated, wondering whether to tell Venetia her news, but saw that her twin had something of her own on her mind. 'What is it?'

'We only seem to see each other late at night now,' Venetia said with an uneasy smile. 'We don't get to talk.'

'So what do you want to talk about?' Taking off her coat, Ginny dropped it on a chair.

'About Easter.'

'What about it? We're going to stay with Mother as always, aren't we?'

Not answering directly, Venetia said, 'Mother hasn't met Alex yet. I've told her about him on the phone, of course, but naturally she wants to meet him.'

'So where's the problem? Take him there one Sunday or for a weekend.'

'I did suggest that, but Mother's busy every weekend for weeks with that job she's taken selling entrance tickets at a museum. The only time she has free is Easter. So she suggested that we all three go down.'

Ginny's face set as she realised what Venetia was getting at. 'But Alex has refused to go if I'm going to be there.'

'Yes. Sorry. But he's quite adamant about it.'

Her face pale, she managed to shrug and say, 'The two of you had better go on your own, then. I'll make some excuse to Mother and go some other time.'

Getting to her feet, Venetia said, 'But how about if Alex and I go on the Friday and Saturday, and you go on the Sunday and Monday? And afterwards,' she flushed a little, 'Alex and I intend to go away for a week or so.'

Yes, he would be eager to do that. Ginny remembered how he had brought up the subject when *she'd* been with him. Glancing at her sister's reddened cheeks, Ginny knew that Venetia hadn't yet been to bed with Alex. And she wouldn't be able to at their mother's house so this holiday would be the first time for her. 'Yes, OK. We'll do whatever you want.'

'Thanks.' Venetia put a hand on her arm in quick gratitude and Ginny saw again the engagement ring that Alex had given her. It was in the shape of an 'S' set with small diamonds and with two sapphires in the curves. Seeing the ring, knowing what it meant, hurt unbearably.

Turning abruptly away, Ginny said, 'I have something to tell you, too.' And she told Venetia all about the job that Simon had got her.

'A new perfume! Why, that's wonderful. You must be thrilled,' her twin exclaimed.

'Yes, of course.' And part of Ginny—her mind and her ambition—was thrilled that she'd been so fortunate. The other part—her heart, her emotions—felt completely dead.

They discussed it for a little time, then, when there was nothing more to say, Venetia, in a very reluctant voice said, 'Alex wants us to get married in June. That's one of the reasons why he wants to go and meet Mother soon. He thought I'd like to be married from Mother's house rather than here. And you have to have the banns called and everything.'

'You're going to have a white wedding?'

'Yes.' Venetia smiled. 'Alex insists on it.'

'I see.' A picture of Venetia in a wedding dress with Alex at her side came into Ginny's mind. She bit the inside of her lip, pressing hard to stop the tears. 'That will be nice for you. I'd better start saving up for a present.'

'Alex has asked Jeff to be his best man.'

'Of course. Who else?' Ginny stiffened. 'I suppose Alex has said he doesn't want me there, either.'

'Yes, he has,' Venetia admitted. Her chin came up. 'But I told him you were the person I loved most in the world next to him and that you're going to be at my wedding, whether he liked it or not. And not just there, but as my bridesmaid. I couldn't think of getting married without you being there.'

'Oh, Venetia!' Ginny ran to sit beside her twin on the sofa and they put their arms round each other, both promptly bursting into tears. 'I don't want to spoil it for you,' Ginny said, sobbing. 'I won't go if Alex insists.'

'It will be spoilt if you don't go. I've so missed you these last couple of weeks. I hate it when we're not friends.'

'It was my fault. I'm sorry.'

'No, it was mine in the first place. I've been a bitch,' Venetia confessed through her tears. 'I wanted Alex from the moment I saw him and I was determined to get him.'

'Well, you have, even though I played that trick on you—and on him. Don't ever let him find out that it was me he spent the night with, will you, Venetia?'

'No, of course not.' Her sister looked at her with troubled eyes. 'But I'm terrified I'll give myself away. Is there—is there anything I should know about that night? Anything you did that Alex might want me to do?' Her voice trailed off as she looked away.

Every moment of that night was etched in Ginny's memory but it was too precious to share. So she shook her head firmly. 'No, there's nothing special you should know. Just be yourself. You'll be OK.'

Venetia looked a little relieved. She smiled and dried her eyes. 'Don't let's ever be angry with each other again. I don't think I could bear it.'

'No, OK.' Ginny squeezed her hands. 'We'd better go to bed. We'll both look like death in the morning.'

Things were better and easier between them after that. But for Ginny their renewed compatibility had a dark side, because Venetia couldn't help but talk to her about her wedding plans. Luckily, though, there was only a week to Easter, and Ginny comforted herself with the thought that afterwards she would be away working on the new perfume publicity campaign most of the time. And their mother had been longing for the day when one of them would get married, so Venetia would have her to discuss plans with instead.

Alex had arranged to pick Venetia up on Friday morning before driving on to their mother's house in Cheltenham. The weather looked a little unsettled but it was dry and bright when Ginny went out for her usual morning jog, although she hardly needed to; unhappiness had made her lose weight over the last weeks. She set out later than usual, having helped Venetia to choose clothes to take from their joint wardrobe, and had left her sister hastily pressing the creases out of a skirt she simply had to take with her. The park was busy today; children were on holiday from school as well as adults from work, and the place was rapidly filling with runners, playing children, and walked dogs. Another jogger whom she knew by sight stopped her and said that he and some others were organising a fun-run in aid of charity—would she like to take part? Ginny explained that she was unable to commit herself because of her work schedule but the man wrote the details down for her. Another pair of runners, a married couple, came along halfway through and also had to be told. They all introduced themselves and the couple invited Ginny and the other jogger back for coffee later that morning, which she accepted.

Ginny turned to run on, but they had spent so much time talking that the sky had darkened and soon erupted into a regular April shower. It had to happen in a part of the park where there weren't any trees to shelter under! Ginny ran on but was only wearing a thin T-shirt over tracksuit trousers and was soaked through by the time she reached the trees. Deciding that she was so wet already that she might as well keep going, she ran for home. If anything, it began to rain harder, pelting down in huge drops. Ginny's T-shirt was sticking to her, outlining the soft roundness of her bra-less breasts, and her hair, which she was wearing loose, clung to her head, accentuating the fragile lines of her face.

The shower stopped as suddenly as it had begun and the sun came out again. Leaving the park, Ginny reached the road. Steam rose from the wet pavement. She ran across the road, brushing the hair out of her eyes to see. There were cars parked on both sides of the street but she didn't notice them, intent on getting home. There was quite a high wall outside their building with a pillared entrance that had once had a gate but was now open. Ginny turned quickly into it, her foot slid on the wet York stone path and she gave a yelp of pain as she fell—straight into Alex's arms!

He was carrying Venetia's suitcase but automatically dropped it to catch her. 'What the hell?'

He didn't recognise her immediately but then she said, 'Oh, my ankle.'

'Ginny?' His body began to stiffen and he let her go.

She put a hand on the gatepost to steady herself, then hopped round and leant against it. Trickles of rain ran down her face and her lips were parted, half in pain, half in amazement and joy at being held in Alex's arms again even for a moment. Her eyes flew to his face, loving him, longing for him. Alex's eyes went over her, saw her body through the thin, wet shirt and darkened with desire.

They both saw it, recognised it, in the same moment. Ginny gave a small gasp, filled with a sudden surge of radiant happiness. But Alex dragged his eyes quickly away from her, the skin around his mouth going white with shock at his own reaction. Turning, he picked up the case and carried it out to his car, parked a little way down the street. He took longer over it than he should have done, but when he came back Ginny was still leaning against the gatepost.

'I'm sorry, Alex, but you'll have to help me. I think I've twisted my ankle.'

He gave her a searching, wary look, but then his brows flickered and he came to slowly put his arm round her waist and help her to stand upright. 'Put your arm round my neck,' he ordered roughly.

Half carrying her, he helped her inside and up the stairs into the flat, depositing her on a chair. Ginny looked round. 'Where's Venetia?'

'She dropped the Easter egg she'd bought for your mother and it broke, so she went rushing out to buy another. And some flowers, I think.' He gave her a brooding look, noting how she was lying back against the cushion and the pinched look in her face. 'Is that ankle hurting you?' And, when Ginny nodded, he reluctantly said, 'I'd better take a look at it.'

'It doesn't matter.' Ginny made a wry face. 'I've got a couple of days to rest it.'

But Alex squatted down and took off her shoe and then her sock. His touch was firm and yet gentle, and Ginny would have given a great deal to have stayed like that for the rest of her life. As it was she winced when he ran his fingers over the ankle.

'I don't think it's too bad,' he told her, his voice as cold and detached as he could make it. 'As you say, a couple of days' rest will probably put it right. But it will help if I put an ice-pack on it.'

He went into the kitchen and Ginny relaxed against the cushions. Alex might be cold to her now, but he had wanted her, back there at the gate. Even though he was in love with Venetia, for a few wonderful seconds he had wanted *her*. That he could do so had startled and embarrassed him, but it had happened nevertheless. She could hear Alex moving around in the kitchen, could imagine what it would be like if it were her he loved. Ginny closed her eyes tightly, afraid that she might cry and give herself away, but two tears managed to creep between her lashes and trickle down her cheeks just as he came back.

Kneeling down in front of her, Alex put the ice-pack round her ankle, tying it in place with a clean towel. That done, he glanced up at her and saw the tears glistening on her lashes. 'I'm sorry if I hurt you,' he said shortly.

Ginny shook her head helplessly. 'No, you've been very kind.' Lifting her hand, she brushed away the tears. 'Sorry.'

He stood up and she guessed that he hated to see her cry. She was his enemy and enemies weren't supposed to be so vulnerable. 'You ought to get those wet things off,' he said awkwardly.

'Yes, I suppose so.' In a mercurial change of mood, she felt an inner flash of amusement, knowing that if it had been Venetia he would have had her in her bedroom and her wet clothes stripped off like a shot. As it was, she grinned and said, 'If you'll help me into my room I'll be able to manage the rest.'

At the sight of her smile Alex's features eased a little. Reaching down, he helped her to her feet and put his arm round her again. 'You're being very brave,' he remarked.

'Oh, sure,' Ginny retorted with a bitter little laugh. 'That's what Jeff called me—the bravest woman he knows.'

Standing still, Alex gave her a puzzled frown. 'Why should he say that?'

'What?' Ginny flushed beetroot-red. 'Oh, just because of—of something that happened.' Then, quickly, 'Look, do we have to stand here? I'd like to go and rest this ankle.'

'Of course.' He helped her into her bedroom, fetched her a towel from the bathroom and left her alone.

When Venetia came home ten minutes later Ginny was sitting on the bed drying her hair. She wanted to know how it happened and fussed round, getting Ginny some fresh clothes and wanting to blow-dry her hair.

'No,' Ginny protested, taking the drier from her. 'Alex is waiting for you. Go on, get going.'

'But what about food and everything? How will you manage?'

'There's loads in the freezer. I shall be fine. Now go, woman.'

Venetia laughed. 'OK, see you a week on Sunday.'

'Mm.' Reaching out, Ginny caught her twin's hand. 'And good luck when you—on Saturday night.'

Venetia bent to give her a quick kiss, her face flushed. 'Thanks. Take a sleeping pill, will you? I don't want to share it.' Then she turned and hurried away.

They'd been gone for some time before Ginny remembered that she was supposed to be having coffee with the couple she'd met in the park. Finding their number in the phone book, she rang and explained the situation, and ended up with everyone coming round to her instead.

Surprisingly, Friday and Saturday passed quite pleasantly. Her ankle improved rapidly, especially when she strapped it up with a sports bandage, and by Saturday afternoon she was able to put her weight on it. She had been worried that she might not be able to drive to her mother's on Sunday, but it felt so much better that she decided to go. During the two days Ginny caught up with a lot of mending and reading and watched hours of television, desperately trying to keep her mind occupied and not think of Venetia and

Alex. Venetia rang from their mother's on Friday evening to ask how her ankle was, and she spoke to her again on Saturday afternoon when Ginny phoned to say she would be well enough to drive down.

'We'll be leaving about six,' Venetia told her. 'We're driving down to the coast, to stay at a hotel near Quinmouth.'

Ginny wished Venetia hadn't told her that; she didn't want any facts to help embroider her already vivid imagination. At eight Ginny made herself something to eat, but as the evening wore on became more and more restless, her twin's nervousness coming through. At ten, remembering what Venetia had advised, she took a sleeping pill and rolled into bed, almost immediately falling asleep despite her inner tension.

Whenever one of them was alone in the flat, she always made a point of taking the phone into the bedroom with her. Ginny had done so automatically but cursed when it dragged her awake from a deep sleep only, it seemed, two minutes later. Ginny groped for the light and groaned when she saw that it was one in the morning. She reached for the phone but, before she'd picked it up, already knew that it was her twin and that Venetia was in trouble.

'What is it?' She spoke sharply, although her brain was so muzzy that it wouldn't function properly.

'Oh, Ginny, you've got to come down here. The most dreadful thing has happened.' Venetia's voice was high and hysterical.

'You've had an accident,' Ginny said in terrible foreboding.

'No. But——' Venetia broke off, choked by terrible sobs and it was a few agonising moments before she managed to gasp out, 'Oh, Ginny. Alex has found out the truth. He knows that it was you he made love to and not me!'

CHAPTER EIGHT

Even as she sped along through empty streets and almost deserted motorways Ginny knew that she would never forget that terrible drive through the night. Venetia had become almost incoherent on the phone, crying, and saying over and over again that Alex would never forgive her, and all Ginny had managed to get out of her was the name and address of the hotel.

'Venetia, listen to me,' she ordered sharply, trying to cut through her sister's hysteria. 'Is Alex there?'

'No. He—he walked out.' Venetia broke into a fresh flood of tears.

'All right. Just sit tight till I get there. I'll be as quick as I can. And if Alex comes back try to keep him there. Venetia? Did you hear?'

'Yes. But please get here quickly, Ginny. I don't know what to do, what to say to him.'

Her twin's plea echoed in Ginny's ears as she tore through the darkness, pushing the speed-limit and just praying that there were no police cars on watch. Venetia must somehow have given away their secret, but how she couldn't think. Not that it really mattered; all that mattered now was that Alex must be going through hell. And her poor sister, too. And Ginny had to get there and try and put things right. If that was possible. If Alex would even listen to her.

The patrol tank light on the dashboard flashed a warning and she had some anxious moments until she

reached a service area and was able to fill the tank.
Ginny took the opportunity to study the map and
found that she still had quite a distance to go, even
though she was making such good time. She had got
dressed in such a rush that she had forgotten to put
the bandage back on her ankle and it was starting to
ache. Ignoring it, Ginny pressed on along the
motorway, torn by anxiety but thanking her stars that
she had a decent car for the journey. Thanks to Alex,
of course. Although he could never in his wildest
imaginings have thought that it would be put to this
use.

Ginny tried to concentrate entirely on her driving,
but the roads were so empty that her mind couldn't
help straying to that hotel by the sea that Alex had
chosen for his romantic holiday. There must have been
a terrible scene when he'd found out. Ginny cringed
inwardly at the thought of Alex's fury. And poor
Venetia had had to take it all, when it wasn't really
her fault. Ginny had no idea what she was going to
do when she got there; if Alex had gone then there
was probably nothing she could do except comfort
Venetia and bring her home, then try and contact Alex
later and talk to him. But if he was still there . . . How
the hell did she start to explain to him?

She made such good time that she reached
Quinmouth just before four in the morning, but it
took her another frustrating half-hour of driving
round before she found the hotel. The town was obviously a popular resort with dozens of hotels and no
one about at that time of night to ask. She finally
found it a mile or so outside the town, a converted
Georgian country house standing on a piece of ground
overlooking the sea, with only a discreet sign at the

entrance to the drive which she had missed when she'd first driven past it in the dark.

With a sigh of relief Ginny drove up to the hotel and parked outside. There was a light over the porch but the door was locked when she tried it. Without hesitation, Ginny pulled down the handle of the bell at the side of the door, not caring if she woke every guest in the place.

But it was Venetia who answered it almost at once. Throwing open the door, she rushed into Ginny's arms, almost knocking her over. 'Oh, Ginny! Ginny.' She burst into a paroxysm of weeping.

'Hush. Hush. Don't worry, I'm here now.' Ginny led her away from the hotel to a seat that she could see on the lawn. Dawn was beginning to break but there was a mist that clung to the garden, making the air feel cold and damp. Letting Venetia cry for some minutes, Ginny comforted her as best she could although it was pretty useless. 'Venetia?' Unable to wait any longer, Ginny gave her twin a little shake. 'Venetia, what happened?'

'It was terrible.' Venetia straightened up and looked at Ginny with pain-filled eyes. 'I thought he was going to kill me.'

'Did he hurt you?' Ginny asked in dismay.

'No. But the way he looked at me. What he said.' Venetia shuddered in remembered horror.

'But I don't understand. How did he find out? What did you do?'

'I didn't do anything. He——'

'But you must have done,' Ginny broke in vehemently. 'You must have given yourself away.'

'*No*. Everything—everything was going fine. We had dinner and then we—we went for a walk by the sea before we went back to our room. It was all—just perfect. Wonderful.' Venetia started to cry again, deep, heartbroken sobs.

'Hush now. *So what happened?*' Ginny demanded, unable to control her impatience.

'Alex—he left a lamp on. But when he started to undress me he—he ... Oh, God, Ginny, he saw that I had an appendix scar. And you hadn't.'

'Oh, no!' Ginny's eyes widened in horror. 'Oh, God, I never thought of that! But you had it done so long ago that I'd forgotten clean about it. Oh, what a fool I've been. Venetia, I'm so sorry. What did you do?'

'I tried to brazen it out. I told him he'd made a mistake. But that only made things worse. He knew right away that it must have been you he went to bed with. And he was so furious. But he was so—so cold. He said ...' She gave another great sob. 'He said he supposed we had found it very amusing to switch places. And he wanted to know how often we had done it. And he—he wanted to know which one of us it was now.'

'Oh, hell,' Ginny murmured on an agonised breath. 'Now what are we going to do?' She turned back to Venetia. 'You say he left?'

'Yes. He just slammed out of the room. But he—he hasn't gone away. He left all his things and his car keys behind. I've got the keys here in my pocket.' She held them up. 'I thought that if I kept them he wouldn't be able to leave. That we might still have a chance to ...'

'Well done.' Ginny gave her a hug. 'But he hasn't come back yet?'

'No.'

'He must have gone for a walk.' Ginny looked round, almost as if she expected to see Alex in the rapidly lightening garden.

Venetia shivered and Ginny put her arms round her again. 'You're cold. Come on, I'll take you up to your room. Quiet now, we don't want anyone to see us.'

It was a beautiful room, high-ceilinged and with a four-poster bed hung with soft draperies. A fairy-tale setting for Alex and the woman he loved. His things were still there, as Venetia had said: his jacket on the press, his wallet on the table beside the bed. Good, he couldn't get very far without that.

There were tea-making facilities in the room. Ginny made them both a hot drink but took only a few sips of her own before she set it down and said abruptly, 'I'm going to look for Alex. If I find him I'll try and explain, put things right.'

Venetia looked up. 'For which of us?' she asked hollowly.

'I don't know,' Ginny said honestly. 'He probably won't want either of us. But I will be acting for us both. If I don't find him and he comes back, open your curtains and leave the light on so that I'll see it.'

'The room faces the sea,' Venetia reminded her dully.

'All right.' Ginny hesitated, trying to find some words to encourage her twin, but was unable to think of any.

Reading her mind, Venetia said in a heart-broken voice, 'He hates me. He hates us both; I saw it in his eyes.'

'Perhaps. But he was very much in love, too. We'll just have to hope that love is the stronger.'

The hotel was still silent as Ginny crept down the main staircase and let herself out, leaving the door on the latch. Maybe Alex hadn't come back because the door had been locked, although she couldn't see that stopping him any more than it had her. Walking round to the other side of the building, Ginny was almost dazzled by the sun as it rose above the distant horizon of the sea. It was going to be a beautiful day. Great rays of red and gold filled the sky, giving the earth the beauty that it must have had on the very first dawn of time. But Ginny put her hand up to impatiently screen her eyes from the sun. She must find Alex.

She tried to think what she would have done in his place, and headed instinctively for the sea. There was a flight of wide wooden steps leading down from the garden at the back of the hotel to the beach. Ginny went down them and felt a stab of pain from her ankle, but it was better on the sand. She looked from side to side, wondering which way Alex would have gone. Undecided, she walked nearer to the sea, trying to see further along the beach, then noticed a set of footprints going off to the right. They were a man's footprints, taking long, deep, angry strides, made after the tide had receded and left the beach clean. There was just the one set of footprints, so he hadn't yet come back, at least not that way. Turning to the right, Ginny set off to look for Alex, wishing that she could run, but going as fast as she could with her painful ankle.

After about half a mile, the beach curved away into a wide bay with a promontory at the far end, and it was here that she found Alex some twenty minutes later. He was sitting on a rock above the tide line,

elbows resting on his knees, his chin on his hands,
gazing out to sea. He was wearing jeans and a
navy sweater, beach shoes on his feet. He must have
seen her coming but he made no move to leave, which
was something. Ginny was limping by the time she
reached the rocks. Putting a hand on the stone to rest
for a moment, she found it warm to her touch.

Alex looked down at her. 'What the hell do you
want?' His voice was coldly contemptuous.

'To—to talk. Shall I come up or will you come
down?'

He didn't answer, turning away, so after a moment
Ginny began to climb up to join him.

It took her several minutes; the rocks were uneven
and slippery at the base with seaweed that smelt
strongly in the sun. A smell that took her back to
childhood holidays with Venetia. Times when they had
been happy, before their parents had split up. As
Ginny reached Alex's rock at last she looked at the
coldness of his averted profile and wondered sadly
whether either of them would ever be happy again.

There was a higher rock behind them; Ginny leaned
against it, getting her breath back, trying to think what
to say. One thing was for sure: Alex certainly wasn't
going to help her. His back was firmly towards her
and around him there was a wall of anger so intense
that she could almost see it. Realising that only di-
rectness would penetrate it, she said clearly, 'It wasn't
done out of amusement. It was done out of love.'

Alex didn't react for a moment, then he turned and
laughed. It as the harshest, bleakest sound Ginny had
ever heard. 'Love?' He spat the word out.

'Yes. My love for you. I know that it was wrong
and I shouldn't have let things go that far, but——'

'Just a moment,' Alex cut in icily. 'Just who are you?'

'I'm Ginny,' she faltered.

'Thank you. It's nice to know who I'm dealing with—although I have no guarantee, of course, that you're not lying again.' His voice had such a sarcastic edge that each word felt like the cut of a razor-sharp blade.

Ginny winced and took a deep breath. 'I know that you're terribly angry and you have every right to be. But I'd like to explain. We didn't set out to fool you or anything. Or at least Venetia didn't. Well, she did at first but I——'

Alex's eyes darkened with scarcely controlled rage. 'For God's sake! Just say what you've got to say or else get the hell away from here.'

'All right. I'm sorry. I—it started when we met on the plane. I was the one you met, not Venetia.'

His head came up at that and Alex stared at her. 'Is that true?'

'*Yes.*' Ginny looked steadily into his eyes, willing him to believe her. After a moment he nodded, and she went on, 'But your letter looking for me went to Venetia. We have the same initials, you see, and——'

'But she knew about me,' Alex objected.

'Yes, I'd told her on the phone that I'd met you. As I was still away she went along to meet you instead and of course you thought she was me. And she— she didn't enlighten you because she immediately fell for you, just—just as I had done.'

Alex shot her a piercing look. 'And when you came back?'

'By that time you'd been out with Venetia several times and had made it plain that you were keen on her. I wanted her to—to give you up, but she wouldn't. We had a row about it.'

'And if she had given me up and you'd taken *her* place, would you have told me about it?' Ginny bit her lip and looked away. Alex gave another sardonic laugh. 'I thought not. You're both a pair of little cheats.'

'I don't know!' Ginny burst out. 'I probably would have done. Eventually. But I loved you, and I didn't see why I should let Venetia just step in and take you from me.'

'You make me feel like a ball between two tennis players,' Alex said, his coldness erupting into a burst of fury. 'Didn't either of you give a damn about *my* feelings?'

'Yes, of course. I tried to tell you. But when I told you I was jealous you thought it was because you were coming between Venetia and me. And then you got angry with me and I knew that you wouldn't believe me if I told you the truth.'

'So why didn't you come right out and say it if that was how you felt, instead of dropping hints that could be misconstrued?'

Ginny sighed. 'I wanted to. But before I was sure that I was in love with you I'd promised Venetia that I wouldn't tell you about her taking my place.' She gave Alex an unhappy look. 'I'm sorry, but Venetia loves you, too, you see.'

He gave her a bleak, glaring look, then said, dragging the question out, his voice raw with hurt, 'And just which one of you did I go to bed with?'

Ginny's face drained of colour. 'That was me.'

'Oh, really? And how did you choose? By tossing a coin to see which of you was to be the first? That's usually what you do when you have a choice, isn't it? Toss a coin?'

'No.' She looked away, her voice husky. 'I fooled Venetia into going away, then I phoned you and said that her shoot had been cancelled. I'd tried so hard to give you up for Venetia's sake, but I—I never stopped hoping that you'd one day realise that it had been me you met on the plane. I thought that if I went out with you, if we talked together, that you might—might . . .' Her voice broke. 'And that night you said that you thought you'd fallen in love with me then, on the plane. I think that was the most wonderful moment of my life. No, not quite the most wonderful.' She raised her eyes, dark and vulnerable, to look into his. 'That came later when you made love to me.' Lowering her head again, Ginny went on, 'You made it plain that you wanted to go to bed with me— Venetia, and I couldn't tell you the truth then. I wanted you so much. And—and I knew that if I told you you would have ended it there and then.'

She paused, close to tears, and Alex said sharply, a sneer in his voice. 'You're right. So that was what all the play-acting was about—so that I wouldn't call you by Venetia's name.' He said it half to himself, but there was scorn in his tone as he said, 'Well, go on. You can't stop there. Why didn't you tell me the following morning? Surely you must have been confident enough of me to tell me then?'

Her head came up at last and Ginny spoke with a note of pride in her voice that had the persuasion of sincerity. 'It was the most wonderful night of my life. I knew that if I told you who I was it would be tarnished and cheapened for both of us. I didn't want that. I couldn't spoil things by telling you. I knew that night would be a memory I could hold on to for the rest of my life. And I wanted it to be that for you, too—even if you did think you had spent it with Venetia.'

Alex stared at her, read the love in her eyes. 'You did that for Venetia?'

Ginny shook her head. 'No, I did it for you. Only for you.'

'So that's why Jeff said you were brave.' His body stiffened. 'For him to say that he must know the truth.'

With a reluctant nod, Ginny admitted. 'Yes. Venetia rang you at home that night and Jeff answered. When you didn't come home he guessed what must have happened.'

'And didn't tell me,' Alex said on a murderous note.

'He wanted to, but I made him promise not to. We all hoped you would never find out.'

'Well, thank you very much. My friend, my fiancée, and—what do I call you . . . my mistress?—all getting together to save me from knowing that I've been deceived and lied to. And all for my own good, as if I'm not man enough to take it.' His tone was infinitely contemptuous. Getting to his feet, Alex stood towering over her. 'But I'm quite capable of telling the lot of you to go to hell. And the next time you decide to play your cheap little tricks on some other dupe just remember that you're not entirely identical.' And he sprang nimbly down from the rocks and began to walk back along the beach.

'Alex, wait! Please help me down. I can't manage with my ankle.'

She didn't think he was going to stop, and she had to call again before he reluctantly turned and came back, angry that he had to help her.

When she stood beside him on the sand, Ginny caught his sleeve before he could walk away again. 'Alex, Venetia is the innocent one in all this; I'm the one to blame. She loves you so much and she's so upset. Please, won't you at least go and see her, talk to her? And then you'll be——'

'No, I damn well won't,' Alex said viciously. 'The way I feel now I never want to see either of you again. You're both as bad as the other. You've both lied and cheated, so how am I supposed to trust either of you again?' He gave her a scorching look. 'Does it occur to you that now I don't even know which of you I was in love with? How the hell am I supposed to feel about that, let alone sort it out in my mind?'

Shaking off her arm, he began to stride back up the beach. Ginny hobbled after him, cursing her injured ankle, afraid that he would get back to the hotel and force Venetia to give him his car keys. And once he left she was sure that neither of them would ever see him again. But Alex had only gone a hundred yards or so before he glanced back and saw her limping along behind him. With an oath, he turned round and came back. 'You should never have tried to walk on that ankle. I suppose you drove here as well?'

'I had to. You—Venetia needed me.'

He gave her a look that spoke volumes but swung her up in his arms and carried her back along the half-mile of beach. Ginny put her arms around his neck, her heart thumping, but she held herself stiffly, knowing that just to touch him tenderly, as she longed

to do, would immediately alienate him. He carried
her all the way up the steps to the terraced garden that
overlooked the sea, then set her down. 'Where's
Venetia?' he demanded brusquely.

'In your room, waiting for you.'

She looked at him with anxious, pleading eyes. For
a moment his gaze held hers and he looked as if he
was about to say something, but then he swung away
and walked round the side of the hotel. Ginny stayed
where she was. She had done as much as she could;
now it was up to Venetia.

But her twin came running out to join her only a
couple of minutes later. Ginny had been leaning
against the wall, the sun on her back, but straightened
quickly. 'What happened?'

'He sent me away. I think it was seeing the bed
and—and remembering. He just told me to get the
hell out,' Venetia said with a sob. 'I hoped you'd been
able to persuade him.'

'I tried. But he's so angry that he doesn't want to
know. He said that he doesn't know which one of us
he was in love with.'

'He wasn't in love with *one* of us,' Venetia said on
a sudden bitter note. 'He was in love with us both.'

Ginny nodded. 'Yes, but I don't think he's realised
that yet.'

'Is there no chance?' Venetia said unhappily.

Ginny was about to shrug helplessly when a thought
came to her. 'Maybe there is just a chance. He said
that the way he feels *now*, he never wants to see either
of us again.'

Venetia's face immediately filled with hope.
'Perhaps if we stayed away from him for a while, gave

him a chance to simmer down, and then—and then asked him to choose between us.'

Shaking her head decisively, Ginny said, 'No, that would never work, not with Alex. I'm sure that if he leaves today he'll just write us both off as a nasty experience that he's well out of and we'll never see him again.'

'So there *is* no chance,' Venetia said, deflated.

But Ginny said, 'Do you still have his car keys?'

'Yes.' Venetia tapped her pocket. 'Why?'

'One of us could go and sit in his car and wait for him. Refuse to leave. It's a long ride back to London. Surely in that time he can be convinced that it was only done out of love? And he does love—one of us. That can't all be lost overnight.' Ginny looked into Venetia's anxious eyes. 'It might work. It has to work.'

'He'll be furiously angry.'

'Yes, but he won't be able to refuse to take one of us home, especially if the other has already taken our car and left.' Ginny looked up at the hotel. 'We'll have to hurry, though. He's only got to pack and pay the bill.'

'All right, we'll try it,' Venetia said excitedly. 'We have nothing to lose.' But then her excitement suddenly faded. 'But which one of us will it be?'

Ginny gave her a steady look. 'We have a straight choice; an attempt to get Alex back, or a career in modelling that looks as if it's definitely going to take off.'

They looked at each other, knowing that they both wanted the same thing.

'We'll have to toss for it,' Venetia said slowly.

'Alex won't like that.'

'What other choice do we have?'

Ginny sighed. 'None, I suppose.' She glanced up at the windows again, aware that they must hurry, even though this was to be the most momentous point in their lives. 'But let's get the rules sorted out first. Whoever wins gets to try and get Alex back. The loser must take the modelling career and go right away, never—never see Alex again. I think we have to assure him of that or he'll never be happy.'

Venetia's eyes widened then grew shadowed. 'We can't not see each other ever again.'

'There's only room for one of us in Alex's life. If we win him back then we lose each other. It has to be that way.'

'It isn't fair!' Venetia burst out.

'It was inevitable from the moment you first took my place.'

They looked at each other, feeling a terrible sense of loss and sadness, but then Venetia fished in her pocket and took out a coin, a copper-coloured two-pence piece. 'I'll toss, you call.' It was the way they had always done it, a rule laid down by their father because Venetia was the eldest, even if only by a few minutes. 'Ready?'

Ginny gulped and nodded. The coin went flying up into the air, spinning over and over. 'Heads,' Ginny called on a hoarse, rasping note of dread and anticipation.

The coin came down, spun a little and then settled on the ground where a ray of sunlight caught it, turning it into bright, dazzling gold. Ginny had closed her eyes for a moment, and when she opened them she looked straight into Venetia's. Instinctively she held out her hand and gripped her twin's. Then they bent to look at the coin.

Who has won the toss of the coin?
To conclude this gripping story, look out for
Sally Wentworth's GHOST OF THE PAST,
out next month.

Next month's Romances

Each month, you can choose from a world of variety in romance with Mills & Boon. These are the new titles to look out for next month.

TEMPESTUOUS REUNION Lynne Graham

A CURE FOR LOVE Penny Jordan

UNDERCOVER AFFAIR Lilian Peake

GHOST OF THE PAST Sally Wentworth

ISTANBUL AFFAIR Joanna Mansell

ROARKE'S KINGDOM Sandra Marton

WHEN LOVE RETURNS Vanessa Grant

DANGEROUS INFATUATION Stephanie Howard

LETHAL ATTRACTION Rebecca King

STORMY RELATIONSHIP Margaret Mayo

HONG KONG HONEYMOON Lee Wilkinson

CONTRACT TO LOVE Kate Proctor

WINTER DESTINY Grace Green

AFRICAN ASSIGNMENT Carol Gregor

THE CHALK LINE Kate Walker

STARSIGN

HUNTED HEART Kristy McCallum

Available from Boots, Martins, John Menzies, W.H. Smith and other paperback stockists.

Also available from Mills and Boon Reader Service, P.O. Box 236, Thornton Road, Croydon, Surrey CR9 3RU.

TWIN TORMENT

Please tick the appropriate box for each question.

☑

Did you enjoy reading "TWIN TORMENT" by Sally Wentworth?

Very Much		Not very Much	
Quite a Lot		Not at all	

What did you think of the ending to this book? _____

_____

There will be a sequel to "TWIN TORMENT" called "GHOST OF THE PAST". How likely are you to read it?

Very Likely		Not very Likely	
Quite Likely		Not at all Likely	

Would you like to read more Romances that are linked in this way?

Very Much		Not very Much	
Quite a Lot		Not at all	

Do you have any further comments to make about "TWIN TORMENT"?

_____

6 Which of the following series do you read?

M&B Romances		Silhouette Special Edition	
M&B Best Sellers		Silhouette Desire	
M&B Temptation		Silhouette Sensation	
M&B Medical Romances		Zebra	
M&B Collection		Loveswept	
M&B Masquerade			

7 Where did you get this book from?

M&B Reader Service ☐   New from the shops ☐

Other (please specify): _____

8 Which age group are you?

16-24		45-54	
25-34		55-64	
35-44		65+	

9 What is your occupation? _____

10 Are you a Reader Service subscriber?   Yes ☐   No ☐

If yes please add your subscription number _____

NO STAMP NEEDED   Send to: Mills & Boon Reader Service
FREEPOST, P.O. Box 236, Croydon, Surrey, CR9 9EL.

THANK YOU FOR YOUR HELP

Name: _____   T

Address: _____

_____

_____ Postcode _____